Raw Deal

An Amber Farrell Novella
Prequel to the Bite Back series

I0456904

by
Mark Henwick

Published by *Marque*

Series schedule, reviews & news on
www.athanate.com

Bite Back prequel : Raw Deal
ISBN: 978-0-9573746-7-6

Published in May 2014 by Marque

Mark Henwick asserts the right to be identified as the author of
this work.

ACKNOWLEDGMENTS

It seemed harder producing a novella than a novel! My thanks to all who worked with me.

The cover image team: Chris Mann, Maria Askew and Gideon Henwick.

My major feedback readers: Jessica, Gail, Leiah, TK, Nori.

My editor: Lauren Sweet.

And, without which nothing, my wife and family.

Chris Mann : www.chrismannphotography.co.uk/ - photographer, actor
Gideon Henwick : www.GideonHenwick.com – digital artist
Lauren Sweet : www.LaurenSweet.com – author, editor
Maria Askew : www.MariaAskew.co.uk – actor, model

Email Mark@Athanate.com to request
an email alert when a book is published

Reviews, schedules & news on
www.athanate.com
and
http://www.facebook.com/TheBiteBackSeries

Chapter 1

FRIDAY

"This is Car 148, we got a 510, southbound Broadway, passing Colfax," the radio squawked.

Cars racing. Better than nothing on a slow night. I grabbed the mike before Officer Knight reacted. To be fair, a coffee in one hand and a donut in the other slowed him down.

"This is Car 152, on Humboldt. I'll make Broadway and 7th in one minute."

I swung the Ford Crown Vic around and let the tires talk to me as I hustled us back to cut them off. At least there wasn't much traffic to worry about in Denver at 4 a.m.

"You said one minute, Farrell," Knight said, dumping his coffee overboard. He switched on the lights and grabbed the chicken grip. "Not five seconds."

Pussy.

He took the mike. "Car 152," he said. "Requesting a buddy to help block at Broadway and 7th."

"Car 142, oh sh—" The call broke off for a second. "We have a 480! 480! Broadway and 13th."

Shit, it'd gotten serious quickly. Somehow, one of the racers had found someone to hit.

"Suspect vehicle has turned east on 11th. Car 142 in pursuit, 148 stopped to provide assistance. Requesting ambulance, Broadway and 13th."

12th Avenue. I turned hard, tires shrieking protest.

Knight joined them. "What the fuck? Quit hot dogging," he yelled. "This isn't a friggin' TV show."

"Relax, Knight. I've been trained to handle vehicles at high speeds," I said. And my reflexes were a couple of notches above those of normal people. To be fair, Knight had no way of knowing that, but I wished he'd stop acting like I was your average wet-behind-the-ears police rookie. My military training had given me a clear sense of my own abilities and limitations, and the sooner he learned to trust me, the better partners we'd be.

"On 11th, passing Harrison," came from the radio. That was Wilcox in Car 142.

We passed Harrison on 12th. I knew what the racer was going to try next. And Knight and I were going to be there to stop him. Thankfully, Knight had decided to shut up and let me drive.

"Turning service road, west of Gerritsen," Wilcox said.

Right on cue.

"Shit! He's hitting dumpsters," Wilcox said. "We're blocked. We're blocked."

I slammed on the brakes and hauled the car, screeching and slipping, around into the southern end of the service road.

"Fuck!" Knight yelled, bracing for a crash. It didn't come. The headlights hurtling toward us in the alley suddenly dived as the racer braked heavily and skidded to a halt, the nose slewing to one side. The doors opened and two guys piled out.

Gotcha!

"This is the police," Knight was saying through the bullhorn. "Come out with—"

I was out of the car and running before he finished his sentence. The alley was long and dimly lit, with plenty of cover from the overturned dumpsters. If these dirtbags were armed and we let them establish a defensible position, they'd be invisible and we'd be silhouetted against the light as we tried to come in. Not to mention all the apartment windows lining the alley—an invitation for stray bullets. But if I could stay close enough, the perps would either have to keep moving and get picked up by Wilcox and his partner, or stop and give me the chance to take them down hand-to-hand. Which I was more than happy to do.

The racers were picked out in our headlights. A tall, skinny guy, with sweats hanging halfway off his ass, fell over the trunk and scrambled mindlessly back up the alley to get away. The driver was a different story entirely—he had a compact, athletic build and he was trotting backwards, head up and looking around, hood up to keep his face hidden. When he saw me coming, though, he abandoned caution and took off.

"Hold it, Farrell," Knight called out after me. He wanted to do this by the book. There wasn't time. It was things like this that made me really miss the instinctive understanding of my old special forces team.

I leapt, hit the hood of the racers' car at full stretch and kicked off, launching myself into the air. Beanpole, for all his frenzied scrabbling, had been outdistanced by his partner. He heard me land behind him and turned, shocked I had gotten so close, so quickly.

Surprise!

I didn't give him time to get over it. I shoulder-charged him against a dumpster, winding him. Sweeping his legs out and dropping him to the ground, I had the cuffs on him before he got enough breath back to even think about struggling.

There was no sign of the driver ahead. Knight was coming up behind me, framed in the headlights.

"Wilcox," I said into my radio. "One of them is heading back toward you, on foot."

I heard Wilcox yell, cut off by the flat sound of a shot echoing up the alley.

Crap. That wasn't Wilcox or his partner shooting.

I vaulted the dumpster and sprinted into the darkness. Knight could handle Beanpole, and it'd mean he wasn't standing silhouetted in the lights.

The alley was a mess. The racers had sideswiped over half the dumpsters and they'd either spun around and rolled into the middle, or overturned and spilled their contents onto the road. The smell was overpowering.

The driver was scaling a chain-link fence about halfway down. No sign of a gun. Or a hoodie, for that matter.

I jumped up and hauled him back by his belt. He landed on the balls of his feet, balanced and not at all giving up, especially when he saw he'd been caught by a woman.

Unlike other areas, people underestimating my hand-to-hand skills *never* gets old.

I let his punch slide past me, guiding his momentum with one hand, feeding a little more into his rotation and pulling him off balance. Then I kicked him hard in the back of his knee. As he crumpled, I followed him down, twisting his arm behind his back.

It didn't take him long to figure out that struggling would only dislocate his shoulder.

I didn't have any more cuffs, but Knight or Wilcox would get here eventually and I passed the time by reminding my prisoner that even he had some rights.

He chose to remain silent. Probably thinking how to spin it to his homies when they found out he'd been taken down by a girl.

There was no sign of his gun.

Knight arrived with Beanpole in tow and cuffed the driver just as Wilcox and his partner crept in cautiously, guns drawn. I spared a glance to check that their fingers weren't on the triggers and then set about searching for the driver's missing gun.

As I clambered over dumpsters, I saw that Wilcox was claiming the suspects. That was fine by me; they were the ones that witnessed the hit-and-run.

Besides, they took them in, they did the paperwork.

Ha!

Wilcox clapped Knight on the shoulder. Good ole boys.

With my face hidden, I allowed myself one standard roll of the eyes and a small snort. The praise would be for both of us. Of course.

Denver PD had a lot of good police officers, and Wilcox and Knight weren't bad at all. They were solid. They were the kind of guys that would always turn up to the inter-departmental ballgames, they'd always buy their round in the bar, and they'd always make time to drop in on the grieving family. But they had a strong view of how things should be.

Their view included the sort of role rookies should fill. With my background and training, I didn't fit that role. It made it uncomfortable for both sides.

I shook my head. No point in worrying about that now. I stepped up onto an upended dumpster to shine my flashlight into the tall, upright one behind it.

There was a hoodie inside. Out of reach, of course.

I climbed in gingerly. The driver was dumb enough to take a shot at a policeman, but not so dumb as to be caught holding the gun. I took a photo with a pocket camera and then opened the bundle with a pen, careful not to touch the material. He had stripped his hoodie and his gloves off, wrapped them around the gun and tossed it. Not so clever.

He might have kept his hands clean of gunshot residue that way, but there would be DNA all over this stuff.

I called Knight. "Got the gun here."

He came over and didn't offer to get in the dumpster with me, so I marked it for CSI and began to carefully make my way out.

I could tell by the silence from Knight that he wasn't happy with the way things had gone tonight, but it was about to get worse.

The largest dumpster that had been knocked over was right behind the one I was getting out of. The trash from it had spilled up against a wall. There was something odd about the shapes that made in the shadows. Instead of getting out the way I'd gotten in, I scrambled out of the back onto the large dumpster. Peering over the edge, I shone my flashlight at the spillage and stiffened.

"Knight! Over here."

I jumped down.

Almost hidden beneath the trash was a human hand.

I pulled out a fresh set of latex gloves, snapping them on.

The hand was male, the flesh cool beneath my fingers. I swept the trash from the arm, following it up to the shoulder and neck. He lay on his back, his face contorted in an expression of pain, the eyes staring.

I felt for the neck pulse, knowing it wouldn't be there.

Knight arrived, picking his way through mounds of trash, flashlight beam bobbing as he hopped over the worst of it. "Jeez, Farrell, what now?" he said. The light caught the corpse's face and he sucked in his breath. "Ah, Christ," he muttered. "What a fuckin' night."

Our beams cross-lit the corpse's head and my hand came away from his neck.

"Oh, shit," I said, and rocked back on my heels.

The man's neck had a pattern of gashes that sent a flare of shock through my body. They were deep stab wounds, triangular in shape, as if made by a small ice ax. The flesh around them was as bloodless as supermarket chicken. And the wounds came in evenly-spaced pairs.

"What?" Knight said. He followed my gaze. "Shit," he echoed. "What the hell happened to him?"

I was hoping I didn't know.

I'd spent a year looking for evidence like this in Denver, but I realized in that moment that I'd never really expected to find any.

And you don't know that you've found any now, I lectured myself. I could hear the scathing comment of my old special ops instructor: *Unverified reports are worse than nothing.*

I played my flashlight over the rest of the body and the garbage that still hid most of it. There was almost no blood I could see. I leaned forward as if I was examining the wounds more closely. I was trying to catch the lingering scent that would confirm my suspicions, but the stench of the garbage was overwhelming everything.

"Farrell!" Knight snapped. "Quit screwing around. Tape both the scenes and keep the lists until we get some help."

He moved around, shepherding me away from the body. He was already talking to the dispatcher on his radio, calling in CSI, Homicide and more uniform backup.

He had a point. Nobody wanted me to examine the body before CSI got here. I'd have to get back to it later. Meanwhile, I was the rookie in Car 152, and for all his faults, I had to respect that Knight took his mentoring seriously. If only he could manage to remember that I'd handled more life-or-death situations than a dozen police officers combined.

Or maybe he did remember. Maybe that was the problem.

I taped off the alley at both ends and got two crime scene forms from the patrol car—one for the dead body and one for the racers' car. I took up my post and waited for the crime scene crows to gather.

I'd lived around death for ten years in the army's most covert and lethal special operations battalion. A body was a body, and I had seen plenty. The problem was, this might not be just another body. If this turned out to be a vampire kill, then I had a responsibility to report it—and not to the Denver PD.

Another couple of patrols arrived to help secure the site, leaving me the south end of the alley, next to my patrol car.

"You okay?" Knight said, ducking under the tape to come join me.

I turned. "I'm fine. Thanks."

He scuffed his feet, folded his arms and leaned back against the hood of the Crown Vic.

I knew it was coming and I wasn't patient enough to wait for it.

"Something on your mind?" I said.

He snorted without any humor at all.

"You have to ask?" he said. "You went barreling down that alley without even stopping to think. Those guys could've been armed." He paused for obvious effect. "Oh, wait, they *were* armed." He rolled his eyes. "You can thank God they decided to shoot at the veteran cop who had sense enough to find cover, and not at you, bounding over cars and dumpsters like Spidergirl."

I opened my mouth to answer, but he held up his hand and went on. "It's only by blind dumb luck we don't have two stiffs in this alley. Do you know how much paperwork I'd have to do if you got yourself killed?"

Underneath the scathing tone, I could sense real concern. I stopped myself just in time, before I blasted him with a Sergeant Farrell tirade. Instead, I took a deep breath, and then explained my line of reasoning for following the suspects down the alley.

Knight pursed his lips, studying me. "And you were totally confident in your ability to take down both guys?"

I'd served in an unconventional unit, and my training had been unconventional to match, not to mention brutal and thorough. I had no doubts about my ability, but Knight didn't know the full extent of my training, and confidentiality rules meant I couldn't tell him the details.

"I was going to leave you one," I said, trying to make light of it. "Then he started shooting at Wilcox. But, hey, we got both of them, in the alley, with the car and the gun."

"They weren't going to get away, for Christ's sake," he said, waving at the alley. "And there's a good reason we work in pairs. It's safer. It's not just your ass on the line, there are situations where it's safer for both of us if we go in together."

I didn't agree with his comment about them not getting away—the shooter would have been over the fence if I'd been much slower. There *were* situations where it would have been safer and more efficient to work as a pair, but this wasn't one of them. I'd trained in tougher schools than he had and threat assessment was wired into me.

I knew that, but I also knew better than to say it out loud. It would sound like lack of respect for *his* skills and judgment.

"Well, Wilcox thought it was okay. I saw him congratulating you."

I saw you taking the praise. For both of us.

"Y'know what Wilcox was saying to me?" Knight looked down at his boots and I realized not all his anger was directed at me. "He said we were showboating, shaping up to be a pair of real cowboys. Said it was obviously catching."

Crap. I had completely misread what was going on. Knight wasn't being an ass because I'd shown him up.

"You could have set him straight on who did the showboating," I said.

"I'm not the rookie with ambitions," he said. "Wilcox trying to label me a cowboy isn't going to wash with the sergeant. But if it sticks on you, it might end up in your review."

He didn't need to go on. A cowboy was a maverick police officer, someone destined to be shuffled off into a backroom job because no one trusted them. It wasn't a fair assessment, but if it stuck, getting rid of it was something else. Meanwhile, Knight was trying to divert some of the crap from me, not sucking up praise as I'd thought.

"So, maybe Wilcox is full of it," he went on. "Maybe you know what you're doing better than you get credit for, but, y'know, we're not working well together at the moment."

That wasn't good. Unfortunately, I didn't get time to discuss it before we were interrupted by the first arrival.

A car pulled up and a man got out and headed into the alley. Medium height, heavy blond hair with a curl that needed flicking to keep it off his forehead. Sharp jaw. Worked out too much, with too much emphasis on the shoulders and arms. Kinda heavy on his feet. Known to me.

I raised a hand to stop him anyway and got the badge wave in return. He didn't even look at me as he signed the form and walked on. Detective Buchanan was too important to look at uniforms.

Right after him, a couple from CSI turned up and signed in too. The intense blond woman I'd seen before, but her lanky, male partner was new to me.

I got to hand over the crime scene form to one of the other uniforms while CSI took Knight and me inside the tape to do a walk through. My boot mark in the middle of the car's hood got a twitch of eyebrows and I could see the woman mentally measuring the distance to where I'd taken the first racer down. We moved on to the fence, and I glossed over how far ahead of the others I'd got. Knight didn't dispute it. Hopefully, the CSI document on the sequence of events would make us look less like cowboys, and Knight and me more like partners.

At the first dumpster, I gave them the photo I'd taken before opening the hoodie, then we finally moved to the body in the second dumpster. I handed over my latex gloves, which I'd turned inside out, and explained clearing the trash and the pulse check I'd done on the body.

They didn't let me get anywhere near it, and the garbage smell was still killing anything else, so I ended up back outside the tape, still unsure of what had killed the man, but a little happier about Knight.

When the sergeant had first handed out the schedule and I saw I was assigned to partner Knight, about the only thing I'd known about him was that his nickname was 'Silent.' As in huge joke. As in ceaseless patter while I drove.

But he was a decent guy. He didn't smell and he hadn't hit on me. At least, not yet. It's not that I expect it. At five-ten, I'm too tall for a lot of guys. I run a lot, I practice martial arts and I spent years in the army. I don't do simpering. Most guys don't look beyond that, at the auburn hair and green eyes, a product of mixed Celtic and Arapaho blood. I was nothing to write home about, but I'd heard that long hours sharing a cruiser made anyone attractive.

Anyone? I glanced back at Knight and hid a smile.

No. Not gonna work for me.

It wasn't that I needed him specifically as a partner, but I needed a partner, and I needed one who would vouch for me. There were no official forms for that kind of evaluation. But one evening at the bar, someone would ask Knight how the rookie was shaping up, and it was amazing how much a career depended on the answer to that question.

I'd expected hazing and grunt work while I was a rookie, and I could deal with both. But I'd thought all my Ops experience would be an asset. If it turned out to be a liability, I was so screwed.

There was much more at stake for me here than just a job with the police. After the 'incident,' as the army referred to it, they had discharged me and gotten me this job, but they had a price. I was still reporting to them. If I stayed sane, employed, and didn't turn into anything that went bump in the night, I got to stay in Denver. If I failed in any of those areas, they'd reach out and pull me back in.

The city started to wake up, and one of the other uniform guys spelled me so I could fetch coffees.

When I came back, miracles had happened. Buchanan was talking to uniform. Crap.

He swung around as I approached. "Good of you to join us. I hope it's not inconvenient for us to talk during your break."

"Of course not, Detective." I shut myself up before I added *–glad you could make the time for us.*

Even so, Buchanan's jaw worked.

Way to go, Farrell.

I hadn't learned that attitude in the army and it really wouldn't do me any favors here. He was being an asshole, but I couldn't afford to piss him off enough that the others wouldn't back me up. They didn't need to create enemies in their jobs over some smartass rookie who might talk her way out of hers.

"You were first to the body?" he asked.

"Yes. The vehicle over there hit the dumpsters—"

"I'm aware of the background," he cut me off. "You checked he was dead?"

"Yes. No pulse in the throat."

"Did you inform CSI you contaminated their scene?"

Yet another cop who thought I was wet behind the ears. "No, Detective. But I handed them the gloves I wore and explained what I'd done."

Buchanan's eyes narrowed. I looked back innocently.

The Medical Examiner and CSI teams came over and Buchanan turned his back on us. A couple of the ME's assistants wheeled the body into their van. I looked wistfully after it, but I was pretty sure that if I tried to sneak in the van and get a sniff of the corpse, I'd be fired on the spot.

The woman from CSI seemed almost as excluded from Buchanan's conversation as the rest of us. What was her name? Melissa something. Melissa Owen?

I edged over to her. We hadn't been dismissed by Buchanan, but he hadn't told us we had to stand there like dummies.

"Hi, er...Melissa." We had been introduced before, and Owen sounded wrong.

"Amber," she said, turning toward me, her face neutral but open.

"Strange neck wounds on that body."

"Yes."

"Were they the cause of death?"

"Possibly."

"I didn't see any blood in the trash or on the ground nearby."

"Hmmm."

I'd have more luck squeezing stones. I tried a different approach. "Would it be possible for me to have another look?"

"Are you being serious? Along with everything else, you have crime scene investigation experience?" Buchanan's tone dripped sarcasm, cutting across any response that Melissa might have made.

No, I didn't. But I had plenty of experience with dead bodies, and some experience with vampire bites. If that's what these were, then the army was going to want to know about it. Looking out for vampires was the reason I was here and not back where the army could keep a better eye on me. The trouble was, when you spent half your time looking for things that most people thought didn't exist, there was always the chance that you'd start seeing things that weren't there.

A body was bled out. It had a pattern of wounds to the throat. There was no blood around. That wasn't conclusive evidence of vampires, or anything else.

"If we're all finished," said Buchanan, staring at me. "First estimate puts this guy being killed between 10 and 12 last night. He wasn't killed here in the alley or in the apartment building, so the body had to have been brought in from somewhere. I need you to do a house to house within a block to check if anyone saw something between 10 p.m. and the time you got here. Any questions?"

"There's a HALO camera across the way," I said. Denver's HALO surveillance network was intended to reduce crime.

If the camera was on and if it was pointed in this direction, we could have a lead.

"If there're no questions, then I suggest you get on with your task," Buchanan said and walked away. The other two uniforms headed up to where the alley joined 11th Avenue without a word. Even the CSI and ME crew looked suspiciously at me as they left.

"Oh, nice work, *Detective* Farrell." Knight jerked his head and we walked back past our patrol car. "I thought you wanted to try for Homicide eventually."

"I do." I looked to the heavens. "Don't try and tell me that asshole is responsible for admission."

"No." Knight shook his head. "He's not responsible. But he goes to ball games with the guy who is."

I groaned. That wasn't what I wanted to hear, on top of a graveyard shift patrol and the promise of a long extra stretch of getting told nothing by the people living nearby. We split up and started knocking on doors.

A time of death of 11 p.m., give or take. Of course, I didn't know it then, but that was when the clock had started ticking.

Chapter 2

A couple of hours later, and with nothing to show for it, I pushed open the door to a shoe shop of some kind, the last place on my section.

There were racks of shoes and a workbench on the left, where a large man with a bushy beard was carefully packing some beautiful cowboy boots into a box. An intoxicating smell of fresh brewed coffee wafted from the back of the shop, fighting against the scent of freshly treated leather.

The man looked up at me over little, half-glass spectacles. "Welcome. Welcome," he boomed, with a heavy German accent. "And for you, I think, these." He put the box aside and brought up another pair of boots onto the worktop.

"Oh, God, I wish," I said. At his nod, I picked one up and turned it over in my hands. It was the kind of quality you can't find in the shopping mall. A handmade boot, the sole arched like a cat stretching and with a silky soft shaft.

I wanted them. My head gave my heart a major talking-to and I put the boot back down on the counter, my fingers reluctant to stop stroking it.

I sighed. "I'm afraid I'm here to ask questions, not to look at boots." I flipped the page of my notebook and wrote the shop name at the top—Schumacher's. The name made me grin.

"Sit, sit. I will answer all your questions. I have nothing to hide." He came out from behind his bench, chuckling and holding his beefy hands up in surrender.

I sat and he put his head through the door to the back.

"Klara. Some coffee please, for this young woman. Are there still cookies?"

I closed my eyes. "Coffee and cookies. If Klara's not your wife, then I'll marry you as soon as I'm off duty."

He laughed, put his glasses aside and sat opposite me.

"I'm Officer Farrell." I smiled. "Amber. Remember, you'll need that for the marriage certificate. And you are?"

"My name is Werner Schumacher. While we talk, I must do this. Please. Your foot, without the shoe."

Bemused, and a little hesitantly, I pulled my right shoe off, rolled up the pant leg and let him guide my foot into a machine sitting on the floor between us. I was pretty sure there was some police regulation against this, but if it got him to talk freely...

"Do you live in this building?" I asked.

"Yes," he said. "Yes, we live upstairs, the three of us. Hold still." He pressed a button and peered down at the machine, which whirred and clicked.

"Were any of you awake between the hours of 10 p.m. and 4 a.m. last night?"

He looked up and blinked. "Last night, after dinner, I worked. Here, behind the bench. Until, oh, eleven."

Klara came in. She was a tiny, energetic woman. The important thing was she was carrying coffee. Real coffee.

"Werner!" she said. "This woman is busy and you are testing your toy on her."

I smiled and waved off her concern, and her offers of creamer and sugar. I let her leave the cookies, though.

"This is important, Mr. Schumacher. Did you see anyone suspicious on the road outside at any time between 10 p.m. and the time you stopped? Any suspicious activity?"

The shop was at the far end of the block from the alley. If the murderer had brought the victim here by car he wouldn't have seen anything, and I was reasonably sure the corpse hadn't been dragged along the sidewalk. In LA maybe, but, hey, this was Denver.

"The other foot, please." He hummed a bit. "Yes. I saw some people that I did not like."

I swapped feet.

"People you know?"

He shook his head and looked down at the machine. I took a sip of Mrs. Schumacher's coffee and got a glorious jolt of pure caffeine.

"Could you describe them?"

"It was dark. I just finish and turn off the lights. Maybe five minutes before eleven." He waggled his hand uncertainly. " I look across the road. One very tall, six foot six inches, perhaps, fair hair. Two shorter men, your height, darker, maybe Mexican. One with a mustache. All with coats to here." He chopped his hand against his thigh. "All collars up." He flicked the collar of his shirt.

I snuck another cookie. "And what was it about them you didn't like?"

He stole one of my cookies and sat back in his seat, thinking and chewing.

"Moving," he said. "The way they are moving. Down the street in the city, but looking like hunters, yes? Looking for someone. Or following someone. Not looking to the side. Not talking. Not pleasant people." He shook his head.

I jotted it down and put my shoes back on. It would just finish my day to have Buchanan walk in here now and see me in my stocking feet. I didn't think this information was relevant, but at least there was someone who had been looking outside at the right time. Maybe he'd seen something else that he would remember later.

"It could also be, I have seen too much of your TV." He shrugged, and spun the little screen on the machine around to show me. "Now look, your feet, here."

The machine had scanned my feet in, and was now displaying them as 3D models, slowly turning around.

"When I make you your boots, I have exact measurements. The fit will be perfect."

"I'm a policewoman, Mr. Schumacher, and I can hardly afford store boots, let alone handmade."

"Store boots!" He snorted. "Rubbish. A waste of money. My boots," he leaned forward, "my boots are an investment."

I laughed. "I need to invest in my car first, but I'm tempted, really I am."

Note to self, go buy a lottery ticket.

"You said there's three of you," I went on. "Who's the third?"

"Our daughter, Emily."

Something in his voice made me glance up from my notes. This had nothing to do with my job here, but the shop was the last one on the block and I needed an excuse to sip some more coffee and nibble the last sweet ginger cookie. "Problem?"

"No, no. Not really." He smiled a little. "Every year, you look back and think the problems from last year weren't so bad, not so?"

"What's this year's problem?"

"Oh, such a little thing really," Klara said, coming back in with the pot. "She and her friends, they dress in black and do the makeup." She indicated around her eyes. "You know, the dark eyes. They call it Goth or Emo. They listen to the ugly music."

She'd brought over a photograph from behind the counter, a young girl with black hair and wide eyes. She had an innocent look I never quite managed at that age, no matter how hard I'd practiced in the mirror.

Back then, I thought I'd get away with things if I looked like that. Now, it just made me wonder what she'd been up to.

"Kids experiment with styles," I said, handing the photo back.

"Did you?" Klara asked.

Actually, I hadn't. When I was not much older than Emily, my dad got sick and died. The insurance company wouldn't pay. Bad things happened. I dropped out of school to help support the family. I joined the army and got expert in ways of killing people.

"No, I was kinda too busy."

I left the Schumachers' shop a short while later, with an invitation to stop in when I was passing and an assurance that there was always coffee and sometimes there were cookies too. I did *not* look at the boots as I went out. I have a will of iron.

And I needed it, to keep from biting Buchanan's idiot head off when we reported back. He took it as an affront that all we'd collected between us was one shoemaker who might have seen three people heading down the street, looking mean.

I tuned him out as he vented, using the time to scan the activity in the alley. The body was long gone—bagged, tagged and on its way to the morgue. I really wished I'd gotten a better look at it.

I was seeing Colonel Laine today—my liaison with the army. The man who I was supposed to report to if I found any credible sign of vampire presence or activity here in Denver. Operative word—credible. I'd seen an unusual pattern of neck wounds and a suspicious lack of blood at the scene, but so far that was inconclusive. I needed solid proof before making any reports; the only thing worse than being the only known person who could identify vampires would be turning into a person who saw vampires when they weren't there.

I'd already managed to piss off my partner, and made an ass of myself in front of the other uniforms here. On top of that, I'd probably persuaded the CSI team I was a morbid lunatic. Buchanan had clearly written me off already. If I brought the army in now and it turned out I was wrong, the whole house of cards would come down.

Strictly speaking, I should have been back at the base right now, under close observation. I'm sure that's what the scientists had recommended. Their version of close observation included restraints and a soundproof cell with no windows.

I'd spent time in that cell. My vocal cords ached with memories; my wrists itched with phantom burns.

I still couldn't quite believe that I'd been let out, even though it had been a year now. Not just let out—I'd been set up with a job. Two, in fact, since I'd blown the first job. Working in the police was my second chance, and common sense said it was also my last chance.

None of it's my goddamn fault!

I stomped on that. I couldn't waste time bitching. This was my reality. Just to keeping standing still, I had to succeed at my police job and I had to meet my obligations to the army. The problem was when they overlapped like this, I could screw up both of them with one false move. And the minute I was no more use to the army out here, I would end up back in that cell. Sweat chilled my forehead. Anything but that.

Knight was herding me back to our patrol car. I wanted to check out the alley and the dumpster again, sniff around for a hint of vampires, but there were still techs crawling around, making notes and bagging garbage. As far as Knight was concerned, I was just rubbernecking, and I'd caused enough problems with him for one day. I drove us back to the station and we clocked out.

I thought about trying to get into the morgue and have a look at that body, but figured I'd already rocked the boat enough for the moment. I could check the reports once the coroner had determined cause of death. Then, if further investigation was warranted, I could make a decision about what to do.

There were more mundane problems as well. I needed to leave some extra time in case I had trouble with my car, and I really needed to get some rest before my meeting with the colonel. These meetings weren't ever easy, and this time I had to hide today's suspicious murder from him until I confirmed it one way or the other.

I had plenty of time to regret those decisions over the next few days.

Chapter 3

I'd set my alarm for an hour's sleep, and it jerked me awake, sending another nightmare slithering back into the pit of my subconscious.

I didn't linger over it. I took a shower, tied my hair back and got dressed. Breakfast was coffee and some fruit to go. I glanced around out of habit to see if there was anything I'd forgotten. Laundry was bagged and ready for a spare moment. My spare police uniform was hanging, ready for my next shift. My handguns were in the safe underneath the bed.

The little apartment was bright and somehow sad. Maybe I needed to get some pictures on the walls. The only things I had out were on my bedside table. Some photos and, of course, Tara's plaque: my twin sister's memorial. It was plain, a glossy stone rectangle the size of a desk photograph, jet black, with cursive gold lettering at the bottom, saying simply *Tara Farrell*. I brushed it with my fingers.

I was delaying. The run-up to every appointment with the colonel was like this: a sick dread that built and built. If I failed any of his tests, answered a question wrong—if he even thought I'd begun to turn—he'd have me hauled back to base without even a chance to say goodbye. He could have a squad waiting right now.

But putting it off wasn't going to help, and being late was unthinkable. That wasn't just my military training; I didn't want to give them any reason to feel they had to come hunting for me. I slipped out, locking the door behind me.

Twenty minutes later I was downtown where the colonel had told me to meet him, in front of the Denver Art Museum.

He was right on time, appearing suddenly around a corner and moving with that deceptively quick stride of his. He was wearing dark pants and shirt, with a pale summer blazer.

"Colonel." We weren't in uniform—I wasn't even in the army now—and I still wanted to salute, damn it.

"Sergeant." His eyes flickered at my twitchy arm. He was calling me by my old rank. It was a compromise; either Amber or Farrell would have sounded odd. Or maybe it was a subtle reminder of our relationship; I wasn't in the army, but I sure as hell still worked for him.

To my surprise, he bought tickets and headed inside. I followed him into the museum's galleries. At that time of the day, there was little chance of being overheard if we kept it down, so maybe it was as good as any other public place.

I'd left school early and joined the army. It wasn't an impulsive decision, more that a whole bunch of circumstances had pushed me that way. I'd vaguely hoped to get into something exciting, but I hadn't even heard of the unit that offered to transfer me from my basic training to a special program. That intrigued me. When I got there, the instructors told me they'd watch me walk out within a month, if they hadn't kicked me out before then. That motivated me.

I loved it. I spent ten years in Ops 4-10, the unit that almost no one, not even the regular army, knew about. We did the high-risk tasks where the US couldn't be seen to be involved, where other channels had failed. Where there was no hope remaining. We acquired strategic information, extracted people and destroyed organizations in areas where, if we were caught, the US would deny all knowledge of us and leave us to our fate.

There was plausible deniability all right; we didn't officially exist.

The colonel had been the commanding officer. He was damned good at that. I'd been damned good at my job, too, until one night I wasn't. I'd lost my entire team, and nearly lost my life. In a way, I *had* lost my life, and was left with this—a tightrope walk between hunting down creatures people didn't believe existed, and being locked up as one.

"How have you been feeling?" he asked.

"I'm fine."

Lie.

I couldn't say anything else. Anything other than 'fine,' and the scientists would start to cover their asses, telling the colonel that I could go crazy and rampage through malls killing children. The colonel must have stuck his neck out to get me out of the cell in the first place, but he would have no choice but to put me back if the scientists got nervous. And once back, they'd never let me out again.

I handed him an envelope of expenses and written reports as a distraction. He slipped it in his folder and passed me back an envelope which would contain a check for my last expenses.

I knew he wouldn't be happy with my answer. He tried the long silence way of getting me to talk, but I'd been there, done that. I'd walk silently through the whole museum and look at every exhibit until his time was up, if necessary.

"It's been a year," he said eventually. "And only a few months since the last job blew up on us. I'm not sure 'fine' quite covers it."

A year. I knew that. I knew it in my bones, in the itch of my throat when I looked at it in the mirror, or in the panic of my nightmares. A year ago, I'd lost my squad, one by one, in the dark jungles of South America. I'd survived. They'd actually bagged me as a corpse—no one could have survived those injuries. Half my throat had been torn out. It must have looked as if there was more blood soaking the dirt around me than remaining in me. But I wasn't dead, and five days later you could hardly see the scars. I was raving and screaming, but I was alive and physically healed.

The army hadn't believed in vampires. And if you were talking Hollywood vampires, they still didn't. Vampires didn't turn to dust when you killed them—I was still clutching my attacker's severed head when they found me. Sunlight and religious artifacts had no effect. But they drank human blood all right, and the army wanted to know if I was going to.

I hadn't yet. I was stable. There were some physical changes: it was harder to injure me, and I healed quickly. My health, strength and stamina had improved. I saw better in the dark than the average person. The army was very, very interested. Or at least, the little part of the army I'd been involved in. No one else knew, and part of the conditions of my 'release' was that it had to stay that way. The drawbacks—the nightmares, the paranoia—those the army weren't so interested in. 'Just Post-Traumatic Stress Disorder. You'll get over it. Oh, and you can't go talk to a head doctor, by the way. Security issues.'

"I'm getting along," I said out loud. "Police work is better than the accounting job." My voice sounded creaky. "I'm finding my feet, and I'm doing everything you asked as well."

The colonel flipped his folder open. "Well, as long as the medical team is happy with your answers, you won't need to come back in for another checkup yet."

Crap. He had to remind me. I'd do pretty much anything to stay away from them, even answer their questions. I'd never been claustrophobic until they'd strapped me to a bed and left me in that tiny room. The only thing that had kept me from screaming and thrashing till I passed out again was that they'd been watching me. Even when they weren't there in person, their cameras had focused cold, unblinking eyes on me, 24/7.

'The subject is distressed...'

One of them had actually said that. The sound of his voice floated out of the maelstrom of memories, cold and detached. I shivered.

I'd found a way to force the reactions back down inside, to show them nothing of what I was feeling. I used that again now, determined not to let the colonel see how rattled I was.

"Nightmares?" he asked abruptly, his pen hovering over a printed list.

"Fewer. The same ones. They're getting real old now," I lied.

"Any other sleep problems?"

"No." That was true. The nightmares didn't leave time for anything else.

"Anxiety, unexplained physiological changes, sensations of heat, cold, racing heart, arrhythmia?"

Like right now.

"None of them," I said.

The colonel paused beside an exhibit.

"Outside of the nightmares," he read from his list, "do you repeatedly visualize or think about events in the army?"

"No," I lied again. I tried to avoid it. I'd loved my life in Ops 4-10 and now I could never go back. Thinking about it was torturing myself. I had to break this habit. This was the new me. Out here, on my own. Standing strong. Not looking back.

"Blackouts?"

Prickles of cold ran down my back. We were heading off the PTSD track. The medical team had theorized that I would experience psychogenic blackouts if my 'condition' progressed.

"No." Not yet. Not ever, I hoped. There would be no repeal if I turned. I'd spend the rest of my life in restraints, being studied by scientists who would dispassionately note down how distressed the subject looked.

The colonel folded the pad under his arm and gazed at the Western scene we'd stopped in front of. I wasn't fooled. There were more questions to answer.

"Are you still running, Sergeant?"

"Yeah. It's not as regular now because of my hours."

"Have your fitness or stamina levels improved unexpectedly?"

"Not unexpectedly," I hedged. "I've been doing a lot of workouts at the police gym and I've also taken up Kung Fu training again. I found a Kwan here, with a good teacher."

Colonel Laine raised an eyebrow. "You're hardly in need of more martial arts training."

"With respect, Colonel, I don't agree. And I'm careful with other students."

He snorted, looked as if he was about to turn away, but came back suddenly, right in my face.

"Cognitive dissonance?" he asked, staring at my eyes. He didn't blink any more than a camera lens would have.

There it was: The Question. The medics had drummed it into me before I'd been allowed out. In order to be a vampire, I'd have to hold different beliefs. I'd have to be able, not just to do previously unthinkable things, like sucking blood, but to *want* to do them. And they theorized that the changeover would be relatively slow. There'd be a time when I'd be halfway, wanting to do something and not wanting to do it at the same time. Seriously screwed in my head. That was their warning flag. They'd have to imprison me. Once I turned completely, there was no knowing what I'd do or how it might end.

No way. Just not going to happen.

"No, sir. I'm stable," I said.

We stayed like that, eyeball to eyeball, for a good minute before he broke away.

Relief flowed through me. I took it I'd passed again and I was still free.

We walked into the next gallery.

"Your searches have all come up blank so far," he said.

I'd been worrying they'd take the lack of progress as a sign I was hiding something from them. Now I was worrying that if I told them about the body in the dumpster and it turned out to be a false alarm, they'd think I was becoming unstable. That I was imagining things. That I needed to be back under observation.

"Yes, but it's a big city, there can't be many of them—"

"And they keep their heads down. We did draw up the projections together." He frowned. "Maybe the underlying assumptions were wrong. Maybe we're looking in the wrong place."

I didn't like the way this was heading. Searching for evidence of vampires in the USA was a major reason I'd been allowed out. Take it away and there would be an argument for returning me to the base and all that went with that.

"I understood it would take time," I said. I was their only detector, and what I used wasn't high tech or reliable. As the vampires had closed in on my squad in the jungle, I'd found I could sense them, in two ways. There was a feeling, like something you knew you'd forgotten as you were about to leave the house, or like the feeling you got when you just knew someone had snuck up and was standing right behind you.

The scientists had rolled their eyes at that. The second way was more to their liking; I could smell vampires. They gave off a sweet, coppery scent. Very few others thought they could smell it—and most of those changed their minds when challenged—but the scientists had been able to measure electrical patterns in my brain when I got a sniff of vampire. They'd used the bodies to provide the smell. They'd been less happy when whatever was causing the smell decayed away and disappeared, but at least they'd managed to verify their results. It was official; I could smell the vampires that had attacked and killed my team.

Smell and spidey-sense had to be the two least reliable methods of detection in a city full of people and its own smells. And I had to support myself with a job; I couldn't spend all my time wandering around sniffing butts. So we'd applied some more assumptions to narrow down the search. People believed vampires didn't exist, so vampires must be very secretive. But if they needed blood, they had to come out sometimes. Clubs and raves and fringe society seemed to be the likeliest places. So here I was, the only person in the world being ordered by the army to live it up in Denver's nightlife. Yay me.

Now, I had my first possible report to make. But my sense of smell had been overwhelmed by the trash, and the rest was inconclusive. I needed more before I raised it with the colonel.

What if I was wrong? Or worse, what if I was right? What would happen once I'd found them their vampires? Would my usefulness be over? Or would I be hauled back to the lab for comparison studies? Either way, I held off.

Instead, he had me go back over my routine reports for the last couple of weeks, just in case there was anything we'd missed. Then he surprised me again.

"I've taken on board some help for you," said the colonel. "An internet specialist is searching the web for places or people in Denver that need to be looked into, so we can become more focused." He pulled a slip of paper out of the folder and handed it to me. "This place seems to check a lot of boxes on our profile, and there's a special event going on tonight."

The paper was a printout from a website for Club Agonia. I'd heard of it, and the images confirmed everything. Whips. Chains. Leather. Handcuffs. Things that I didn't even want to know the use of. I couldn't keep the reaction off my face.

"Uh, Colonel—"

"I'm not asking you to join in, Sergeant. Just have a look at the place, and the owner." He handed me another sheet. "The club is common knowledge; the identity of this person isn't."

The owner was apparently called Dominé. There was a blurry image that could have been anybody, and just the one name, with someone's scrawled instructions on pronunciation—Dom-in-ay.

To hell with the boss. She was hardly likely to be trawling the floor of her club. My problem was with the club itself, and what went on there. How did he expect me to blend in? If he thought I was going to stride in there with a riding crop and a leather bustier, he had another think coming.

I tried again. "Colonel, this is a clique club. You get in by invitation. You get an invitation by joining in."

"Tonight may be different," he said. "There's an event called the Blood Orchid Market. It has a vampire theme." He had to have been laughing inside at this. He passed me another printout, with emailed invitations to the event that his specialist had managed to copy. "There'll be a lot of ordinary people dressed up, but from what we've seen, we think this is worth a visit. I have absolute faith in your ability to get in and have a look. And get out, without getting caught up in whatever's going on. Simple, for a person of your capabilities."

He finished by handing me a slim file, including schematics of the club's layout inside.

Simple. Right.

My night off had just evaporated. At least I hadn't planned anything.

Outside, the colonel made a call and a couple of minutes later, a black car pulled up. He opened the door for me.

"I'm having a van converted for our future meetings. It'll make it more convenient to talk and run the tests," he said as he joined me in the back seat. "Where would you like to be dropped off?"

I gave the address where I'd left my car.

In the meantime, the colonel had done his commanding officer voodoo on me.

Don't give me excuses, just get on with it.

My concerns were not important.

I started planning. Success in this kind of op was all a matter of retaining the initiative. However, from his *simple* requirement, I'd picked up a slew of chores. I'd just have to get around all of them. There wasn't any slack. But at least being busy would stop me from worrying about Club Agonia.

He pressed a button and a security screen slid up between us and the driver.

From a case at his feet, he took out a small box with straps.

My heart rate spiked. *Crap.* I'd known it was coming, but still, crap. I took it, strapped it on my arm and pressed the button.

The colonel had asked the scientists' questions and I had given answers. I didn't know if the scientists even bothered to look at my answers. This, I knew, they paid attention to.

They had found chemicals in my body after my recovery: strings of proteins, which they called prions, for want of a better name. Prion was a name for proteins that caused devastating brain diseases. The prions they found in me hadn't done that, and the working concept was that the prions actually caused vampirism or were an indicator of it. The box measured the level of prions in my blood. If the readout was too high, I wouldn't be getting back out of this car until we reached the base.

The little readout showed 0.40. Higher than the last one. I stopped breathing.

The colonel took the unit back and carefully jotted down the reading.

"Within acceptable variance," he murmured.

I kept my face calm, let my breath out silently, and started to carefully relax some of the muscles that had tensed up.

Keep it all hidden.

The colonel packed the unit away as we arrived beside my car.

"Sergeant, the Observation team has no idea whether there is a psychological or biological trigger for finally becoming a vampire." He sighed. "You're here in Denver for a reason. Don't breach the terms, and so long as the reason remains valid, I'm not going to haul you back in for having nightmares or feeling stressed."

"Thanks, Colonel." Nice sentiments. I gave a small smile and let my guard down. Like hell.

"You really don't think about 4-10?" he said.

"I think about the good times, sometimes."

Another lie. Ops 4-10 was my life for over a third of it. My friends and colleagues, all torn away from me as if they'd all died that night in the jungle. I thought of them a lot.

He looked almost disappointed, but he nodded and I got out. I watched as they drove off.

I hadn't told him how I really felt. I hadn't told him my suspicions about yesterday's murder. Whatever supportive things he said about good reasons, I couldn't afford for him to start thinking I was going flaky, or that the PTSD was out of hand and my paranoia was taking over. I wasn't going to give him any reason to take me back.

As for the murder; time enough to alert him if I found proof.

'You're here in Denver for a reason.' He hadn't been explicit about the catch in that. He'd even sounded sort of supportive, but he had to know I'd thought this through. The army needed me to find vampires. Once I'd found vampires, what else would they need me for? Certainly nothing that left me here in Denver. I could think of lots of things they might want from me, but they all involved being back under observation.

As for the colonel, we'd gotten along well in Ops 4-10. He was in overall command of the unit, and that meant he was where the buck stopped when I'd messed up, gotten my squad killed and gotten myself bitten. He'd lost the Ops 4-10 position and ended up running the small medical Observations team which was investigating me, Obs for short. I could hardly be surprised he wasn't my best friend forever, that he seemed to radiate disappointment in me.

His car turned the corner. I eased the tension out of my shoulders and closed my eyes. This morning had felt too close. I hoped tonight would turn up something that would take the colonel's attention off me.

I should have been more careful what I wished for.

Chapter 4

My first stop was a thrift shop, where I bought a pair of coveralls. Then I had to go chasing for clothes that would suit a visit to Club Agonia's Blood Orchid Market later. That search took me all the way out to Candy's in Boulder. Every mile with the car threatening to stall if I went above forty. After that, I was downright eager to get fixing it.

It took way longer to find a suitable garage than I thought.

I'd bought a ten-year-old Ford from a guy who thought he was selling me a problem, with a price to match. I knew I had a bargain. The engine and drive train were sound. I knew what the problems were and I actually preferred the stick shift. But I needed to replace the alternator and fuel pump, and to do that I needed a proper workplace and tools.

By the time I reached Aurora Car Services, time was running out. The other garages had turned me away or wanted too much. If this one went the same way, I'd lose my chance of doing anything this afternoon, and the problems needed fixing before the car gave up and left me stranded somewhere.

The garage was a small, clean operation with two car bays. One bay was empty—good. There was a Harley outside, a chop job, and well maintained—also good. As I walked in, I noted the tool cabinets, all full but for the tools being used. I hoped I'd get lucky here.

The guy spotted my shoes and emerged from under the Honda he was working on.

"Yeah?"

Not exactly a welcome. His hair was black and wavy-wild, his eyes dark and his chin unshaven. He was about my height, skinny and strong. Tattoos showed at the edges of his coveralls.

"Hi, I'm looking to rent a space to work on my car, and tools."

"What you got and what you doing?"

"Ford Focus. I need to replace the alternator and fuel pump. I should be able to do the alternator today. I'll have to come back for the fuel pump."

"Just you?" he said suspiciously.

I nodded. He thought I was eye candy trying to get a good deal for my boyfriend. Flattering, sort of.

He strolled to the door to look at the car, wiping his hands on a rag. I followed.

"Great bike," I said.

"Thanks. I'm Rom." He stuck a hand out.

"Amber." We shook.

He waved at the empty bay. "Ten dollars an hour. Put the tools back where they come from. Pay for anything you break."

"That's a good price." I couldn't believe it. A frustrating day had made me as suspicious as him.

He shrugged. "I think you gonna have someone watching."

I raised an eyebrow. "I'm not working with my shirt off."

Rom grunted. "Good to hear. Don't want nothing get caught in the engine. You get asked a couple questions, too."

He walked away without saying anything more about it. Take it or leave it.

Damn, I *had* to get started on the car and there was no time to find another garage. Without a replacement alternator, my battery would be dead before I got another day off. I had to risk it. This garage was off the main drag and out of sight. But if whoever wanted to come and watch me fixing my car was going to try something, they'd find that wrenches could be used for twisting all kinds of nuts off.

I quickly had my Focus up in the bay. With my hair tied out of the way and the thrift shop coveralls protecting me, I went to work. I had time, as long as it went without a hitch.

Rom wandered in and out, pretending not to look at the tools I picked and how I was using them. Apparently satisfied, he disappeared back under the Honda.

I'd barely got the coolant tank and steering hydraulics stuff out of the way when I sensed I was being watched from the doorway. She looked about fourteen or fifteen, and shared Rom's gypsy hair and eyes. She was frowning at me. I mentally shrugged and got on with my task. At least, if that was the limit of my audience, I didn't need to be concerned.

As I started to loosen the bolts on the alternator, she appeared beside the car.

I ignored her and while my hands occupied themselves, I visualized the exit doors and fire escapes from Club Agonia. Getting in was a problem I'd yet to solve, but my safety, in the event there was something sinister inside, depended on being able to get out again. What if they had locked the exits—completely against regulations, but something clubs were known to do occasionally. There were large windows on the top floor and skylights. I liked the idea of getting out through skylights, but they would definitely be locked and they were more likely to be toughened glass. Take some explosives in?

"Why you doing that?" the girl asked. It came out as aggressive, in the way shy people sometimes are without meaning to be.

I gave a mental sigh. I needed to focus on my plan for tonight. "Needs fixing," I said, trying for a tone that was off-putting without being downright mean. My fingers kept moving, automatically double-checking that the wrench was sitting neatly on a bolt I couldn't see clearly, before I put any force on it.

With door security at clubs these days, I'd likely be searched. Not a good idea to take a gun in, but there were other weapons I might use.

Out of the corner of my eye, I could see the girl had screwed her face up with that adults-never-understand-me look. "No, why are *you* doing it?"

"Doesn't fix itself," I said. What was it to her who fixed my car?

The bolt was rusted hard and I found a length of pipe to give me better leverage.

"What about your boyfriend?"

Oh, for heaven's sake. She had really come all the way out here to tell me that I was doing men's work? I was close to snapping out a comeback about the 1950s being long over, but then I heard Rom snort with laughter under the Honda.

Ah. This was part of the deal I had agreed to. I stopped working and took a better look at the girl. She had a look I recognized from my Army days—young women yearning for someone to tell them how much bigger their image of themselves could become. It had taken something for her to overcome her shyness to talk to a stranger. The least I could do was stop being so wrapped up in myself. I could almost feel my army instructors watching me. The unit's master sergeant, Top, he'd be standing there in a parade rest, rocking forward onto the balls of his feet and glaring at me.

Just not good enough, Farrell.

I pulled my head out from beneath the hood and looked at her squarely.

"I haven't got a boyfriend, and even if I did, I wouldn't ask him to do it."

From the puzzled look on her face, my answer seemed to create a dozen more questions.

I tapped the alternator with the wrench. "See this part?" She leaned forward and nodded. "That's the alternator. It's supposed to charge up the battery, and this one isn't. If my battery doesn't get charged I can't start the car. It's a simple replacement and I can do it myself."

I could see her thinking that through before she came up with her next question. "Well, how come you know how to do it?"

"I learned in the army. Seemed a useful thing to know." I snorted. "Truth be told, it wasn't an option. Everyone in my unit had to know how to take an engine apart and put it back together again. You didn't get signed off until the instructor had driven it down to town and back. And heaven help you if it broke down."

And, joy, the test cars were Fords like this.

"Women too?" she said.

I nodded.

"All of them?"

"Yup. What's your name?" I asked.

"Jofranka." She looked away, seeming embarrassed at being asked. "Just Jo is fine."

"I'm Amber." I started to put my hand out and then looked at it. Maybe not. But the dirt didn't put her off; she took my hand and shook it hesitantly.

"Is it all right if I ask questions? 'Cos they say I ask too many."

I bit my tongue to stop myself asking where the hell they had gotten that idea from. I kept my face serious as I slid the old alternator out. "I can't promise to answer all of them."

The floodgates opened.

In the cocoon of Ops 4-10, you got on and did what you had to and forgot how some people were outside. Gender wasn't an excuse you could use, nor was it a reason that they'd expect less of you. Jo hadn't had that. She was bright and cheerful, once she stopped being shy, but she just seemed to have picked up a can't-do-that attitude about herself and women in general.

She was Rom's niece, and his house or shop was where she had to spend most of her days when she wasn't at school. I didn't know what her own home life was like, but I got a sense of why Rom wanted her to talk to me and have her see me doing things for myself. I hoped I did some good. I nearly made her miss her bus. She checked when I was going to come back and flew out the door as I was finishing up.

I'd had my head up my backside, worrying about the colonel and what was happening to me. None of that was useful. Jofranka had pulled me out of it and made me feel good about myself. Even Top would have smiled. I hoped she'd be around when I came back to work on the fuel pump.

I put the tools back and dropped the hood.

Rom slid back out from his hiding place under the Honda. He'd been laughing so hard, there were tears on his cheeks.

"Oh, man, you done good! I owe you," he gasped, wiping his face with his forearms.

"Oh, no. We agreed." I handed over the money despite his protests. But a seed of an idea had sprouted earlier. I was missing something for the event at the club tonight; that something was an arrival. I needed to make an impression to be sure I got in.

"Okay," I said, "I'll trade a favor, if you're free later."

"Yeah, can do. What's up?"

"I need to get into a club tonight. It's real difficult, even with the right looks. What I need is to arrive with some drama."

Rom looked over at his pickup, puzzled, but I shook my head and explained what I wanted him to do.

"You sure?" he said.

"Yup. I'll need you to pick me up a block away from the club and drop me off at the door. I'll make my own way back."

"Okay." He laughed again. "Crazy. Deal."

Chapter 5

Being down in Aurora worked out well. Mom lived just a few minutes away, and I was running out of time.

"Mom, hi, can't stop."

"Amber! What a lovely surprise. Are you sure you can't stay for coffee?" I gave her a hug, and she pulled me inside.

"No, I'm sorry, I have—"

"Are you feeling all right? You did hear me say coffee, didn't you?"

"Yes, Mom, but I have to get to the mall before they close."

"And shopping too? There's definitely something wrong. Do you have a fever? Or did you just run out of fruit?"

"*Mom!*" I'm twenty-nine, and I've lived away from home for eleven years, but mothers have some secret magic that turns the clock way back.

"You know, dear, you haven't used that tone with me since you were a teenager. I miss it so." She herded me into the living room and took pity on me. "All right, what is it?"

"You know that pillbox hat and veil you have? Can I borrow it, please?"

"Oh goodness, dressing up, as well? You sit there and I'll call the hospital right now." She smiled at my expression and relented. "I'll go get it."

She returned with the hat, still in its presentation box. It was a sweet little thing with a black net veil hanging halfway down the face. Actually, I wanted to wear it like I wanted to nail it to my head, but it looked the part.

"Off you go, but you're coming for lunch on Sunday. Bring it back then."

"Yes, Mom."

"Good. Then you can tell me all about it. Who was there and so on."

Big emphasis on the 'who.' I was going to have a tough time on Sunday refusing to talk about it. But she'd probably get palpitations if I told her where I'd been, and, of course, I couldn't say why I'd gone there. I'd had ten years of not being able to talk to her about what I did in the army, and she'd almost accepted that. Then, I'd left under circumstances I couldn't tell her about and still, half my life now was secret. And among all the other things, the army wouldn't allow me to get intimate with anyone, in case I was contagious. So, there was no 'who' for me to tell my mother about.

She knew I was holding back, of course.

I watched helplessly as the tension grew, day by day. We were due for an argument. Maybe on Sunday.

I left at a run, and had the pleasure of my mother watching me pull away with the car lurching erratically until the fuel pump picked up.

I barely made it to the Cherry Creek mall in time. The Neumann store had a promotion going on in the cosmetics department. 'Challenge us,' the sign said. 'Give us your face and thirty minutes and we'll give you a new you.'

I intended to take them up on that, if I got there before the cutoff. I could do makeup, of course, I have the double X chromosome. But when I wanted it done right, I got an expert.

"Challenge you," I said, rapping my knuckles on the counter.

The assistant looked at me and then meaningfully at the clock on the wall. By my reckoning, there were thirty minutes and about ten seconds left before closing.

"I'm sorry, ma'am," she said, which meant she wasn't sorry at all, but if she could keep me talking for ten seconds, she could turn me away. Either she wanted to get off work early or she liked the feeling of power she got from refusing me.

Her life was saved by her manager.

"I'll take this," she said, ushering her assistant away and sitting down opposite me with a big box of cosmetics and a broad smile. "Now, what's the look we're going for?"

I couldn't stop myself from glaring. I *so* did not appreciate the irony of this, but I knew I needed to look the part to get into the club tonight.

"Vampire," I said. And I got it. *Angry* vampire.

Chapter 6

Rom was as good as his word. I had half expected he wouldn't show up and I'd have to drive the rest of the way, but I didn't have to worry. Shortly after ten that evening, a block away from Club Agonia, his Harley pulled in behind my parked Ford.

He'd joked he didn't have a chauffeur uniform, but I didn't want that. He was in his heavy biker jacket and studded jeans tucked into steel-toed work boots. His wavy hair was combed back by the wind. Perfect.

"Hey, Amber, you sure 'bout this?" He looked to the side, not meeting my eye. "I asked around. This's not a good place, this club."

"I know. I'm not going there for fun." I patted his arm. "Now, how the hell do we do this?"

In a couple of minutes, we were set. I was wrapped in my long velvet cloak and perched uncomfortably behind him, riding sidesaddle. I had my arms around him, holding tight. I had no intentions on anyone that night, but it felt far too good, feeling his heat soak through my gloves while the seat buzzed me wickedly from below. Motorbikes are real bad news for celibates.

Rom brought the Harley around the block, the engine barely muttering at that speed. As we approached, he twisted the throttle until we got more of a snarl, as if he were going to shoot past. Then he slammed the back brake on and spun us around in the middle of the road with a shriek of tires.

Every head outside the club came up.

I stepped off and casually hit him on the shoulder to dismiss him, as we'd agreed. He gunned the engine and roared back down the road, front wheel lifting clear.

I waited till the sound of the bike died. I'd certainly got their attention. Could I carry this off?

Hell, yeah. I summoned up all the brash confidence I'd learned in Ops 4-10.

I could hear Instructor Ben-Haim's coaching about disguise—*The persona you adopt is a shell, a dead thing, a shadow. Pour yourself into this shell. Your life glows. You light up the persona. You shine through the shell, and people see the persona as a living thing. They don't see you.*

I freaking owned this damn club. I prowled, slowly and deliberately, towards the door, ignoring the line of people waiting hopefully. It was unthinkable that I would join them.

As I came into the light, I eased the cloak open and pushed the hood back. My arms were sheathed in elbow-length black gloves.

The dress I'd found at Candy's was a 1920s knee-length, backless, black cocktail dress with sequins. Beneath that I wore black tights and half-boots. My mom's hat sat to one side of my head and the veil hung down, not obscuring my wonderful vampire makeup at all. I couldn't quite sparkle, if that's what they were expecting, but I slunk up to the door, shimmering in the lights.

Okay, so I lied a little when I spoke to Rom earlier. I hadn't had this much fun in a long time. Being in the police was very worthy, of course. It just wasn't the same as being on a solo mission and all that went with that.

The bouncer silently opened the barrier and I stalked through, letting the cloak float. The mission was green—I was in.

Or so I thought.

I checked the cloak in the lobby and stood for a minute in confusion, looking for a door into the club. I could certainly hear it, but apart from the light in the check-in clerk's cubicle, the lobby was dark. Opposite the cubicle, where I expected the door to be, there was a floor-to-ceiling carved head of a sleeping man, face slack and eyes closed beneath a Neanderthal brow.

On instinct, I walked toward the face. There had to be something there.

As I approached, machinery engaged with a *thunk*. The brow started to rise. Huge eyes opened, staring madly, spilling yellow light over me, and finally the mouth started to gape.

The air from the club wafted out like hot breath, and the noise of the music shook my bones.

I walked forward on the tongue. It was slightly rubbery and wobbly beneath my feet.

Gross.

The throat deposited me right at the edge of the dancing.

The club had a top of the line sound and light system, and the full crowd inside were enjoying themselves. It was exactly what it depicted on the website; it attracted niche clientele and it catered well for them. There was more leather than a whole ranch of cows and enough metalwork in people's faces to make a combine harvester.

I'd been in quieter riots.

The churn of dancers threw a couple against me. They were moving together roughly in time with the music, which was more than I could say for the threesome I bounced off as I staggered back.

A girl with black leather boots up to her crotch and wearing no more than a wide belt as a skirt was stuck between two guys in vampire costumes.

She saw me and flung out a hand. "Hey, pretty vamp, give me a hand here," she yelled. I didn't think she was entirely joking, but she wasn't getting my hand, or any other part of me.

"You got in there, you get yourself out," I yelled back.

"Bitch," she mouthed amiably at me as the guy bit her neck. She wasn't in any particular danger. It was all fake fangs, all pretend and show.

I'd come here for the Blood Orchid Market, and if it was just a vampire theme night at a hot club, that was okay by me.

I fought my way around the crowd and made it to the bar. There were all sorts of scents in here, but nothing that said real vampire to me.

I found a quieter spot eventually and leaned against the bar, sipping a soda.

The whole place was done in black glass: walls, ceiling, even the floor. Expensive, bulletproof glass, the kind they use in the floors of observation towers that people can jump up and down on. Each huge panel was rimmed with shiny steel and seemed to suck light in. The glass gave me the creeps for some reason.

The bar was at the far end from the entrance. In front of me, the dance floor heaved like a herd stampeding. On the right, the DJ was set up against a structure covered in scored metal that reflected lights and shapes.

I pictured the layout of the building.

That structure took up a whole lot of room. The way it came out at an angle above the DJ was odd. Maybe there was a set of stairs inside, going up to the next floor? They hadn't been in the plans the colonel had given me.

There were two more floors. The original stairs had been against the wall, and there was no sign of them now. Okay, so that was almost certainly a set of stairs behind the DJ.

If this was the dance floor, what went on upstairs? If there were vampires in the club, would they come down and dance, or would I need to go up and find them?

I hadn't brought a weapon. Tonight, I was going to rely on running away very quickly if things became dangerous. Down here, there were too many witnesses and plenty of fire exits for anything too dangerous to happen. If there was something going on, it was on the higher floors. It would be guarded and it wouldn't be so easy to pass unnoticed.

And none of this speculation was getting the job done.

I started to make my way through the dancers. If I thought the evening had been peculiar up to then, it went bizarre at that point and never recovered.

A male vampire, another fake, in a Great Gatsby dinner jacket and pleated white shirt, came up and grabbed my arm.

"Take me, please," he shouted over the noise.

"What, right here on the dance floor?"

"No, upstairs." He grimaced in frustration, free hand pushing his slicked hair back down. "You've got the look, I know you'll get in. They just never seem to see me."

I couldn't say I was ignorant of what happened upstairs, but did this guy know? Or did he only think he knew?

"Do you really want to go up there?"

"Of course."

"What do you think goes on?"

"The action, of course." He looked exasperated.

That wasn't especially helpful. He probably didn't know much more than I did. At least it was a sort of confirmation there were people up there. It sounded as if he thought it was just sex. Maybe the worst I could fear tonight was being thrown out for intruding on a private orgy. But much as I appreciated his information, I wasn't taking him with me.

"I've got no invite for me, let alone both of us." I removed his hand and moved away quickly.

He was pulled away by the swirl of dancers. If anything, the floor was getting fuller and rowdier.

There were stairs around the back of the structure; a couple up on a landing, guarding a door, and a big kiss-off sign saying no admittance. The curved steps swept down like descending ripples in a pool. They were made from gleaming pale marble, the sort with big white patterns in it that look like animal fat. The man and woman were lit by a tiny spotlight above them, casting pools of shadow across their faces.

There was no reason for door staff if there really was no admittance allowed. I was lacking a Harley to make an initial impression this time, so it was all going to come down to bluff. And the best bluff, I decided, was to act as if I was doing them a favor.

My foot touched the first step and my nose caught the faintest coppery scent.

Shit!

There had been a part of me that believed this was all nothing more than going through the motions for the colonel, that there were no vampires in Denver. That was wrong.

My heart rate soared and I got a gut-churning flashback of the night when I'd first smelled them in South America.

They were here.

In the same moment, my training kicked in. My brain jerked forward out of the panic freeze. If there were vampires here, they had to be different than those I'd encountered before. For one thing, they had to be very careful not to expose themselves by attacking people. They weren't like the ones I'd fought a year ago in the South American jungle.

My hesitation, with one foot on the first step, did nothing for my attempted disguise of belonging here.

"No admittance," said the woman. She had a European accent I couldn't place, and she was dressed like an eighteenth century gentleman: ruffles oozing out from the collar and cuffs of her stiff velvet jacket. Her head tilted up arrogantly.

"So thoughtful of the management, to provide a speaking sign for illiterates," I said. I forced myself to move up the steps.

Her eyes narrowed in anger, but she looked me over and her face betrayed a hint of uncertainty.

"I'm here for the Blood Orchid," I said, continuing to climb. How many vampires would there be in here? What would they be doing? Would they mark me out immediately? The nearest emergency exit was down the stairs behind me; how quickly could I get out, if I had to?

The man had been leaning against the wall, dressed as an elegant highwayman, with long hair tied back and a Zorro mask. He stood up now, blocking the way.

"Buying or selling?" he said. It sounded rehearsed, a rote phrase. Crap, there was some kind of password. The emails the colonel had shown me hadn't mentioned that.

"I'm from out of town, and I don't *trade*," I said. My heart seemed to be beating in my throat. "I'm here to see what kind of a place Dominé runs."

That was my one ticket to get in—I knew the name of the owner.

Whatever I was doing seemed to be the right thing; now he looked unsure.

"One moment, please."

He pulled out a mike that had been twisted back behind his ear and turned away to talk into it.

I faced the woman. The coppery smell was coming from her, but strangely, there was no feeling of vampire about her. With the adrenaline flooding my system and giving me some false confidence, I moved closer. I was on a level with her now and could look down into her face. Sergeants practice this look, and it has so many uses.

She was nervous, scared even. Her face was half turned away and she was stealing glances at me from beneath her lashes. Given the type of club this was, and the show I was putting on, I guess I shouldn't have been so shocked to realize she was frightened and attracted to me at the same time.

Well, there were two red lights on that. One, I wasn't attracted to her, and two, I wasn't going to give the colonel a reason to snatch me back.

I needed to find out how she came to smell of vampire, and there were probably going to be things I needed to find out about the club. I'd just have to find some way to loosen her tongue when I came out.

I snorted. *No, not what I meant at all!*

The man turned back, interrupting my surreal conversation with myself. I noticed a small camera on a pivot above his head. Someone had gotten an eyeful of me staring down their guards; maybe my bluff was about to be called.

"Ma'am," he said. He stood back against the wall and held the heavy door open. "Straight through the curtains."

Apparently, I looked and acted the part, but now someone inside was aware of me, and probably interested. I'd need to make this quick, before I got thrown out. Or had to beat a retreat.

I took a last, long look at the woman, and then I strode in.

It was about 11. I still didn't know it, but the clock had been ticking for 24 hours, and another person was going to die tonight.

Chapter 7

I passed through the curtains. It was dark inside.

I stepped sideways quickly, my eyes straining to adjust and my body taut with anticipation. I felt too stationary. My training was telling me I might as well have stuck a gun range target on my chest. I sensed people all around me. But no one leaped out of the darkness. And I couldn't smell vampire.

The noise of the dance club was sharply reduced when the door to the stairs closed behind me. I could even hear murmurs in the gloom, laced through with a sort of primal heartbeat from the sound system downstairs.

My arrival had been ignored. Whoever was here wasn't paying me any attention.

I was disoriented by what light there was; there were drapes like veils ahead of me and through them, the floor beyond seemed to glow and pulse, while the ceiling was dark. Between me and the drapes it was darker, but I could sense there were shapes, moving.

I stumbled, instinctively reaching out with a hand.

I touched naked flesh. Rhythmically moving naked flesh. A man groaned.

I snatched my hand back.

All around me, people were making out. On low, bulbous sofas, or floor cushions, or just the floor. What the hell had I expected in a freaking sex club?

I couldn't see well enough, but the sounds didn't suggest anything other than sex, and there was no coppery smell here—I couldn't smell vampire, no, but I could certainly smell the sex.

Someone moaned with pleasure just beside me. A hand brushed against my calf, lingered.

I moved before I got invited to join, edging nervously through the obstacle course, through the gossamer drapes, which were eerie to touch, and into the open space of the upper floor of the club.

I stopped to get my breath back. Up here, the fashion mix from the dance club was reversed.

Here be many vampires. Pretend ones. Still no coppery scent.

There was a bar at the far side, and between me and the bar, the floor was open. It was strobe-lit from below somehow. People swirled across it as if they were dancing in the lights. They would gather in groups, pause and chatter, then the group would dissolve and they'd swirl around some more, like flocks of birds. Everyone seemed to have their head down half the time. I'm not up on all the latest dance moves, but I'd never heard of this one.

The bar seemed to be a better place to stand and look around.

I walked across and finally caught on. I managed not to stumble again, which wouldn't have been cool at all. The floor was glass. I could see the people dancing in the club below me.

I made it to the bar and ordered a rum. Mission rules be damned.

I watched Dominé's inner club members sweep to and fro over the market. One group made a selection, pointing eagerly, and a couple of staff dressed like the two on the door were dispatched to fetch a man and a woman from the dance floor. The group and their selections then disappeared up a staircase at the side of the room. Two guys had a single girl fetched and went to find some space behind the drapes.

I had a better idea than I wanted of what was behind the drapes. What was upstairs?

From the plans I knew there had been rooms up there, but the club had changed since then. Maybe there were bedrooms. Maybe, given the club's kink, there were dungeons. It was too crowded to swing a whip behind the drapes and there hadn't looked to be any kind of place anyone could be strapped down.

I shuddered and then pushed the images aside. I was here on recon, not to judge. And regardless, the dancers who had been selected and come up didn't seem at all upset. On the contrary, they looked as if they regarded it as some sort of a privilege. The club couldn't operate if people disappeared after going upstairs, and it was popular, so I had to guess they still regarded it as a privilege when they came back downstairs.

That didn't necessarily mean there weren't vampires up there.

A mixed group of five came down the stairs and made their way slowly to the bar. They looked sated and tired; a couple of them also looked sore and were moving carefully. No one had any bite marks on their necks.

A couple at the bar saw me watching. She was a curvy redhead, dressed in a black silk pant suit. He was stocky, with fair hair held in a ponytail by a tight steel clip. They were both pretty as magazine covers, skin so pale I wondered if that was cosmetics. While they both stared intently at me, she ran her hand up and down his groin and he casually opened her shirt to caress her breasts. She licked her crimson lips in unmistakable invitation.

Oh crap. I turned away abruptly and gulped the rum. Not just vampires and bouncers to avoid. It was all kinds of fascinating to see, but I had a job to do. I slunk further around the bar, trying to avoid catching anyone's eye.

Staff moved through the club. There were two types: the fetchers and door guards, who were dressed in romantic eighteenth century outfits, and the wait staff, who were dressed in very little. Both sexes of wait staff wore thongs and some kind of collar. The men wore tight cowboy chaps and had made a serious investment in their abs. The women wore short leather basques and I suspected some had made serious investments in their chests. All the wait staff seemed kind of stiff, and I stopped one woman who was passing.

"Your pleasure, mistress?" she whispered, holding her tray in front of her belly.

"Just wanted a better look at you, really," I said.

"Of course." She put her tray behind her and arched her back.

I ignored the display she was putting on. My eyes fixed on her collar. It was made of dull metal, a weave of circles and barbs that dug into the flesh of her neck. No wonder the wait staff moved stiffly.

I looked closer. "That's broken your skin."

"Yes, mistress, it does."

"You're bleeding," I said. She didn't nod—she couldn't really without more pain, but her head moved a little and she smiled. "You like it?" I asked incredulously.

"She does, of course." Another woman slipped between us. "Don't you, Giselle?"

"Yes, Dominé."

French from the sound of her voice, the mysterious Dominé was a small woman, a full head shorter than her employee, whom she held tightly against her.

She offered her face up, inviting a kiss, or demanding it. Giselle had to bend her head. A gasp escaped her as the spikes pierced her flesh. Her eyes darkened and closed.

The kiss was a lingering touch of lips. Then Dominé chuckled and licked Giselle's chest beneath the collar, where a little blood had trickled down. Giselle's breath sighed out.

I backed up, feeling a little nauseous and fighting not to show it.

Dominé hadn't come alone. I could feel others behind me and a glance confirmed two men standing there in the highwayman costumes. Dominé herself was in a black lace dress, a blood-red ribbon in her white hair. A single crimson rose had been embroidered on her dress above her left breast.

Spectacle over, Dominé dismissed Giselle and spun to face me, her eyes bright. "And you, *étranger*, did you enjoy that?"

"Watching you lick some blood from her chest? No, not my scene."

"And what is your scene?"

I said the first thing that came into my head. "Something with a bit more freedom and passion on both sides."

"Ah, yes. Freedom. The *angoisse* is not good for that. However much she enjoys it, it does inhibit movement, even if you take her *debout*, up against a wall. And not just Giselle, of course. All the wait staff are *torquate*. Passion? Well, you find passion where you will."

"You lost me at 'yes'," I said.

She laughed. "I like a person who admits the truth straight off. It saves so much time. Come."

She led the way, and although they didn't actually touch me, her goons shepherded me in her wake.

Her office was behind the bar.

We sat at her desk, silently taking stock of each other. The goons stood by the door.

In the brighter light of her office, I could see that Dominé looked about forty, lean and sharp as a blade. The hair was pure white, but thick and healthy, the skin, pale. Her eyes were gray, cool and depthless, like mountain mist. They missed little and the face was hard.

Her dress was exquisite. It had the look of something handmade. The office was sparse and minimalist, all designer angles, muted metal and frosted glass. This club business paid well.

Another handsome highwayman entered with an ice bucket on a stand, which he placed beside Dominé. He brought two tall fluted glasses from a cabinet, took a bottle of champagne from the ice and eased the cork out with a pop.

The champagne sparkled in the glasses. I wondered about the wisdom of accepting drinks from strangers in bars, but I was distracted by Dominé.

I'd expected her to not bother to acknowledge the presence of her employee. Or, if she were polite, to thank him. Dominé had him bend down and kiss her, very fully. Tongues were involved, or I wasn't a judge. He gave every indication that he enjoyed it and she caressed his cheek fondly before sending him away.

She watched him leave and then turned back to me and toasted me with her glass. We sipped, looking at each other over the rims.

"Do you like the champagne?" she said.

"I'm no expert, but it tastes good to me."

"You drank rum at the bar. Straight rum. An unusual choice."

I shrugged. I liked rum.

Dominé didn't smell of vampire. Not for the first time, I wondered at my ability and how reliable it might be. I had sensed the vampires that had stalked my team in the jungle. I'd caught the barest echoes of that scent at times in Denver, without being able to identify anyone. This evening I'd had my first absolute certainty with the woman on the door, but she wasn't a vampire, she just smelled as if she'd been with one.

But what if different vampires had completely different scents? What if the spidey-sense didn't always work?

What if Dominé was a vampire and I couldn't tell?

She enjoyed trying to shock with her behavior, but that didn't mean anything. I couldn't quite get a handle on her, or her interest in me. I wasn't a member; she could have had me refused entry. Or, if she'd become suspicious I was snooping around, she could have ordered me escorted off the premises. Taking me into her office had sent some kind of a signal and I couldn't figure out whether it was threatening or not.

"Your name?"

"Amber." We could both do the one name bit.

"Hmmm." She tilted her head to one side and regarded me. "Something with more passion, you said, Amber. Like Valerie, perhaps?"

She said it in the French way, with the tone going up at the end.

"Who's Valerie?"

"She's the one on the door tonight. You made quite an impression on her, yet you didn't even exchange names." She clicked her tongue in disapproval.

"Not really my scene either."

"Well." She pouted. "Not interested in this, not interested in that. You've come for the Blood Orchid and you don't trade, as you put it. Club Agonia is for like-minded people, Amber." She leaned forward and rested her chin on one hand. "Tell me, why are you here? What has attracted you to my little club?"

She didn't appear to be some hard-bitten crime lord. On the other hand, she had two big men standing behind me. If I was wrong and she was a vampire, maybe the two men were as well. I wasn't armed and the odds were against me, from what I knew of vampire fighting skills.

But if she was a human and they were just a couple of bouncers, I'd back myself even without weapons. I'm stronger than I look, much quicker and better at fighting than almost anyone expects.

Club Agonia wasn't about drugs or gambling. I'd lay good odds that some of those delicious bodies out there hadn't been born in America and might not have had much in the way of a right to stay, but I hadn't gotten the feeling of anyone being trafficked, or forced, or underage. Yes, Dominé wouldn't want the law looking too closely at what went on. I'm sure the DA could make a case for closing the place, just as I was sure Dominé had a lawyer who could fight it. The police weren't interested in Club Agonia unless something happened or someone made a complaint.

In any event, saying I was a policewoman wouldn't serve any purpose. And Dominé might have more to tell me if I played along. All I had to do was to work out the rules to the game.

"What I was looking for, I haven't found," I said.

"And what was that?"

"I'm looking for the real thing, Dominé. You don't seem to have it. I'm disappointed."

Her face went closed and she made a signal with her hand. I tensed, but all she'd done was order her goons out.

She sat back and stared at me for a long while.

"I thought you looked…" she paused, "predatory, when I saw you on the security camera." She took a deep breath and her gray eyes narrowed with calculation. "And here, before me, you *are* and you *are not*, somehow. The image is not the truth, but neither is the myth."

She seemed to be having the mirror image of my problem evaluating her. Finally, she came to a decision and spoke again. "My Valerie seems to have an attraction to people like you."

I didn't enjoy the implication of what I was like, but I ignored it. "People who are members of your little club? Like-minded people, Dominé?"

She tried to hide it, but a shiver went through her. "No. Not members. People who visited, but are not welcome again."

We drank champagne and stared at each other some more. No one likes to move first in these situations, to be the first to say the unbelievable. I didn't, and yet I knew it wasn't unbelievable at all.

"Club Agonia is much safer, Amber," she said at last. "I sense you are different. These people out there, the ones you seek, you are not like them, exactly. What you want might not be the same. They will not give you a safeword."

She stood and poured more champagne into our glasses. I could see her hand trembled slightly.

"I'm not looking for them to make friends," I said quietly.

Her eyes snapped back to me.

"You are alone." It was almost an accusation.

"Tonight, yes."

She sat back down and frowned in thought for a long time. Then, reaching below, she opened a drawer and took out two simple business cards and a pen. The cards had her singular name, and a telephone number. She handed them to me.

"Please, write a number where I can contact you."

I wrote my cell phone number on one and handed it back.

"What's this for?" I indicated the other card.

"That's for you to keep," she said.

"Why?"

"When you want to come back—" she raised her hand as I started to speak. "When you want to come back, call me. You belong here, Amber. You don't know it yet, but your body does."

I shook my head. "I'm not into pain, or the—"

She interrupted me. "It's not really about pain. It's about passion. And I sense you need passion like a woman in the desert needs water. Trust me…as I find I trust you." She stood up and drained her glass. "As to your task. What I can, I will do. I would take it as a personal favor if you escorted Valerie home tonight. I think she may be too scared to go home on her own. She will meet you in the lobby. There may be something she can say which will help you in your search."

I stood and drained my glass too. Time to go, and I couldn't waste it.

She escorted me as far as the door to her office. She held it open and I walked through.

"*Au revoir*, Amber," she said.

My French just about extended to knowing that meant until we met again.

I wasn't as sure about a lot of what else she'd said, but I wanted to talk to Valerie anyway and she was waiting in the lobby, as Dominé had told me she would be.

"Dominé says I can trust you. She said I can leave now and you'll drive me home." The strange European accent had disappeared, replaced with mid-western. She could barely look me in the eye. She kept her chin down, her face turned to one side.

I nodded.

"You're…" she hesitated, unwilling to say it. "Can I *really* trust you?"

"I'm not like them, Valerie. I can't prove it, but I won't hurt you. And I'll try to make sure no one else does either. I just need to ask you a few questions."

She looked up tentatively. Face on, her eyes looked bruised with worry. Slowly, the tension in her shoulders eased.

"Let me change first. It won't take me a minute."

Before she could move away, I took hold of her chin and gently lifted her jaw up. Her breath caught, but she held still. I slipped a finger into the ruff around her neck and eased the material away from her skin. About halfway down her neck, there were fang marks on both sides.

"We really do need to talk, don't we?" I said. "I'll get the car and pick you up outside."

Chapter 8

We didn't talk in the car. For my part, I was letting it sink in. She was the only other person I'd met who'd been bitten and survived. It gave me a peculiar sense of kinship with her.

I was also taking time trying to work out my strategy. I needed to reassure her, so I had to appear to know exactly what I was talking about while getting every scrap of information out of her. And my thoughts were constantly being shocked back to realizing that I had the first evidence the colonel had sent me to find.

There were vampires in America. Right here in Denver.

And very good at remaining hidden.

To be that, it was surely unthinkable that they'd casually bite someone and then let her go. So what was the deal here? Were they trying to turn her? Or had they been panicked into making a mistake? If it was a mistake, were they going to come back and fix the problem?

And what would that mean—being taken away or being killed?

I had to work this out for Valerie as well as for the colonel.

She lived on Colorado Boulevard, up near City Park.

We pulled up outside an apartment building that made me think Club Agonia paid better than the Denver PD.

She sat, looking intently at the building, making no move to get out.

"Hey," I said, startling her.

"Oh. Sorry. I'm kinda scared."

"It's okay, I'm coming in with you anyway."

"Thanks." She flashed a tight smile and we got out of the car. We must have been an odd sight walking across to the door, Valerie in her jeans and puffy jacket and me in my floaty vampire cloak. It was a shame there was no mist.

Inside, she offered me coffee. I accepted and she walked into a small kitchen area, turning lights on.

"Can I use your bathroom?" I asked. "I want to take the face off."

That got a nervous laugh and a wave down the corridor.

Valerie's apartment was a surprise. I'd expected somewhere scruffy, gloomy and full of angst. Instead, she'd decorated in light pastels and put up real paintings on all the walls, mainly of penguins in funny poses. Everything was spotlessly clean and tidy.

I scrubbed my vampire face away.

A cat greeted me as I came back out, demanding attention loudly.

"I can hear you're meeting Mr. Leo Pardner, the owner of the apartment," Valerie said from the kitchen. "Leo for short. He normally doesn't talk to strangers."

I scratched his ears and he shed hairs on my cloak, buzzing with pleasure.

"Are the penguins your work?" I called out as the coffee machine spluttered to a halt.

"Yeah. I've never seen one really. We watch a lot of wildlife on TV where I come from."

"They're good paintings."

She smiled as she came into the living room with two mugs.

We sat on the sofa and Leo claimed the space between us, which was fine by me.

"Valerie—"

"It's not really Valerie. It's just boring, odd, plain old Valery Hawks from nowhere North Platte, Nebraska." Her name lost the tone at the end when she said it.

I smiled. "Everyone has to come from somewhere. Can't be that bad."

She groaned theatrically and rolled back on the sofa, clutching a cushion to her. "You know they have the biggest rail yard in the world?"

"So?"

"They have a tower specially so you can go see it. You know you're running out of things to do when you climb a tower to go look at a railroad junction."

"Sounds real bad," I agreed.

"And being, well, different... You don't understand." Her eyes flicked to me and away again. She sat up. "Imagine going to school and you're related to a quarter of the people in your class. You go out to eat and get one cousin waiting the table and another cooking the food. You go to a dance and every other partner is a damn cousin. What are you going to do?"

"You can kiss cousins," I pointed out.

"*Not* of the same sex." She put her head in her hands. "Or anyway, not in North Platte."

I chuckled. "Well, you can't be odd *and* boring, and hey, North Platte is sort of exotic for a Denver girl like me."

She glared at me, but without much heat.

"Valerie, being bored is a privilege. Tomorrow, pack up and go home for a while. Please. Take a break." I kept the French pronunciation of her name—it suited her.

"I can't leave Dominé." She saw the expression on my face. "Look, she's been good to me. You don't know what she's really like."

"Hmm. You mean she put on a front for me? Well, people who put on a convincing front usually have a couple more in reserve. Are you sure you've seen her as she really is?"

"Yeah. When she takes you on, she helps you out finding places to stay and getting bank accounts set up, small loans, that sort of thing. And she makes sure we all feel safe. She has those big guys keeping control in case things get out of hand. Kinda have to, I suppose, in a club like ours."

I leaned forward. "Okay, she's probably not as bad as she tries to make out. But she's not good either. And she's miscalculated this time. It's dangerous at the moment. The scars on your neck say it's dangerous. Being scared to walk to your apartment from the parking lot says it's dangerous."

She was scared all right. It barely needed me to push and she was ready to head back to North Platte.

"I'll have to explain to her first," she said.

"Fine. Call in. Explain. Don't tell her where you're going. And don't let her swing some guilt trip on you." I sipped my coffee and went on casually. "Want to tell me about it?"

"I don't..." she stuttered to a halt.

"Valerie, I went through that club tonight and I saw a bunch of people play acting who don't begin to suspect the truth, even in their worst nightmares. I saw a boss who's scared and does suspect the truth. But there were two people there who know the truth and they're both sitting on this sofa."

She nodded jerkily. I could feel the caution that was holding her back dissolve. I leaned forward. If the vampires were that good at staying below the radar, this might be the only chance that came my way. I needed her to give me a good lead.

"They met you at the club?" I prompted.

She took a sip of her coffee and settled back on the sofa, still hugging the cushion to her.

"They came in a couple of times as guests. They aren't members."

"Describe them for me."

"Three of them. All in their twenties or thirties. Rodrigo and Antonio, I reckon come from Mexico. They're built like boxers, not heavyweight, more kinda middleweight, but no scars or busted noses or anything. Rodrigo has a mustache. They both have black hair and dark eyes. The other guy is tall, over six feet. Don't know where he comes from. He's blond, gray eyes, skinny but strong. They call him Raul, but he's not from the same place as them. They're all fit, like they work out."

"They speak English to each other?"

"Sometimes. Other times, a language I never heard before."

"The club let them in, so I guess they were behaving reasonably?"

She nodded.

That made them very different than the ones I'd met.

"Surnames? Addresses?"

She shook her head. Her hand was rubbing her throat and she was staring blankly at the floor.

"So what happened?"

She thought about it. "The first time is kinda blurry, like I was drunk or something." Her lips thinned and she looked over at me. "I don't drink."

"Little recreational smoking?"

She nodded. "Some. Not that night, and it's the wrong sort of feel." She shifted her weight. "Not, y'know, like I was flying. I can't really describe it in words. I think of it like painting. Look, dope is watercolors on soft paper, okay?" I nodded encouragement. "Sex is poster paint. Now imagine you smear that sideways, and you can only just make out what it was before. That's what it feels like in my head."

The cat moved, as if he sensed my disquiet. I stroked him gently.

"Sex?" I asked. There had been people screwing in the club. I tried to keep my question casual. "Did you have sex with any of them?"

"No. It kinda felt like it though." She huffed. "I'm not into guys, but if sex with them was as good as that, I sure as hell would be."

"This was where in the club?"

"They were upstairs in the sofa section. It was early, so the lights were still on. I walked past and I just noticed them somehow, really noticed them. Like they'd called me, but they hadn't."

If I could sense vampires, maybe some other people could, too. I stayed quiet, letting her tell it in her own way.

"I sat down on the arm of the sofa, and talked to them. First off, it was just guy stuff."

"Like what?"

"Oh, they had this joke going. One of them said I was pretty as a picture, he'd hang me on his wall. The next one said I should be in a gallery, and the third one, Rodrigo, told the other two off. But then he said he thought I must have good taste."

I winced.

"I don't think he was making a sick joke then," she said. She finished her coffee. "I said something about feeling they'd called me over. Y'know, just flirting around. They seemed surprised. That's when they started arguing in that language."

"Any idea what it was about?"

"Something about me. Rodrigo wasn't happy I was there. It gets a bit blurry. Next thing I know, I was leaning over Antonio, like we were cuddling. He bit me and there was this feeling. So hot, like I was almost ready to come. Weird or what?"

"He bit you and it didn't hurt at all?" Again, my experience had been different, but I'd been fighting to the death. Valerie's comments about her sensations and the blurring of her memory fit in with a couple of the theories the colonel and I had discussed. If vampires could make humans want to be bitten, that would be dangerous enough, but if they could mess with memories and perceptions—that was a whole different kind of dangerous.

"Yeah." She balled up around the cushion, lowering her face to it. "None of them hurt me." Her voice was muffled. "That time."

I reached out and touched her arm gently. Leo twisted around in a flash and latched onto me with his claws. We burst out laughing and had to fuss him until he let go.

"That night was creepy, but I could live with it," she resumed, when the cat had received enough worship to placate him. "I talked to Dominé. She didn't like the sound of it and she said they wouldn't get in again. But she was out yesterday. Someone let them in. I was on the door to the Sanctum, where you saw me tonight."

She reached behind the sofa, bringing out a huge art folder and putting it on the coffee table. Pinned to the front was a fresh painting. It was done in oils, and looked as if it was still sticky.

Valerie's mouth twisted, as if she felt sick to her stomach.

"I can't remember exactly what happened. But I can remember what it felt like to me," she said, pushing the painting toward me. The intense colors had been spread with a knife, in sharp, straight lines. It was angry, wounded and violent. "I can remember suddenly realizing what they were and being scared shitless. That's the point where things started to happen and it all just gets..." she gestured again at the painting and then pushed the folder away as if she didn't want to be reminded of it. "Marcel was on the door with me. He said nothing happened. He couldn't remember them coming up the stairs at all. They did something to him. Even Dominé didn't believe me until she looked at the recording from the security camera."

Security footage? Hard evidence of vampire activity? I felt goose bumps down my arms.

I'd need that recording from Dominé and I had to get it to the colonel tonight.

"And you, Amber. You're one of them, but you're different. How is that?"

It felt like I'd been gut-punched. All the stuff from Dominé about being like them was so much talk, unsettling but nothing more. Here was a girl who could sense vampires, and she sensed I was one. I'd been sitting here with my Ops 4-10 head on, thinking about nailing vampires in America for the colonel. If I was one too, what did that mean for me?

"What do you mean?" I stalled.

"When you got in my face at the club, I felt the same thing I felt that first night with the three of them. It was as if you'd called out something to me. You're one of them." Leo uncurled and climbed into her arms, butting his head against her chin. "But you're different somehow."

"You're scared of them, but you're not scared of me?"

"I'm not scared of you. Not now. I can't explain. You don't give off the same vibe." She frowned. "You didn't answer."

My lips twitched. No dummy, this one. "I've been bitten. I don't bite."

Valerie thought about this for a while. "If you're not a..." she stumbled over finally saying it, "a vampire, but you've been bitten, does that mean I won't become one either?"

Of course, that was a major reason why she worried, and it was a natural concern.

"I can't say for sure. It's been a year for me, and I'm not a vampire." I shrugged. "I think of it like an infection that my body is fighting."

She thought about that for a while. Leo decided she'd calmed down and he settled on her lap.

"If you're not a vampire," she said, "then why are you looking for them?"

That felt more comfortable for me. *Seem* like a vampire. *Not* a vampire.

"It's something I do."

"Oh my God!" Her eyes lit up. "A real life vampire hunter?" She got up and knelt on the sofa, much to Leo's annoyance. "With stakes and stuff?"

"No stakes, no holy water, no Hollywood."

"But, y'know, the books say the best hunters are part vampire. Does that—"

"The books say a lot of things that aren't true." I ran a hand through my hair. "I hope these guys will vanish and you'll be okay. But while that happens, you need to be in North Platte."

"Message received already." She sat back. "What about the rest of them at the club?"

"You've been bitten and they haven't. I don't care about them."

I didn't really mean that; I was tired and talking carelessly. Valerie didn't like it.

"They're people, Amber. People see they're different and use that as an excuse for all sorts of crap. You can't. You have to understand; you're different, too."

She pulled the art folder back and opened it, leafing through until she found what she was looking for and pulled it out.

"There," she said, putting a painting in front of me. It was beautiful: two angels entwined, male and female, rising out of shadow. Their hands reached up into brilliant sunshine. The female model was Giselle from the club, and she was already beautiful. The male model had a face I'd have had to describe as ugly, but the artist had transformed him with an expression of joy.

"I'm no art critic," I said, "but I'd say it's excellent. Is it yours?"

"No. That's Marcel's work. If I just had a tenth of his talent, I'd be happy."

"Never works like that—"

"I know, I know," she said. "We're never happy if we think like that."

"But anyway, you *are* talented." I waved at the pictures on her walls.

She turned and looked at me grumpily. "I paint funny penguins. I know you say you're not an art critic, so I'll give you a small hint. There's a difference."

I laughed and, after a while, she joined in. It was good to see the tension in her reducing.

But she wasn't finished. "And Giselle." She tapped the painting. "You spoke to her."

"Well, we didn't really speak," I said. "But yes, I met her briefly."

"And because she dresses up in the evening and wears an *angoisse*, she's not worth any concern."

"No—"

"She used to have another job until someone found out she comes to the club. Guess what it was."

I held my hands up in surrender.

"She used to be a teacher. And—"

"Okay, okay." I stopped her. "But my point stands. You've been bitten. They haven't. I want you out of sight. Go back to Nebraska. Visit your parents." I smiled. "Find a discreet cousin."

She snorted.

I leaned back on the sofa. "Does anyone know how to contact you there? Anyone at the club?"

"Only Dominé."

I made a quick decision. I'd gotten about as far as I thought I could with Valerie. Her memory wasn't clear anyway. That security camera footage was what I really needed.

"I'm going back to the club now. I'll get that recording. Stay out of there. Go to Nebraska. One of us will call you."

I got out Dominé's card and had Valerie write her cell phone and landline numbers on the back. I gave her my cell number and said goodbye to Leo, who granted me permission to leave.

At the door, she stopped me, one light hand resting on my arm.

"You're welcome to sleep on the sofa, after you've finished at the club. I have lots of breakfast stuff."

I didn't think the offer was really for the sofa.

"I'm good, thanks. Promise me you'll go?"

"Okay. And thanks."

I drove back to the club. I knew what I was expected to do. I knew what my orders would be.

The colonel had to have Valerie under observation. After all, the same thing had happened to her as happened to me. She might turn. I thought of her painting bright, funny pictures of penguins while locked in the laboratory at the base.

It made me ill.

Chapter 9

If Dominé was surprised to hear from me so soon, she didn't say. I called ahead and despite having scrubbed off my vampire face, I was let straight in and taken to her office. We were left alone.

"There's a security recording of Valerie being bitten, Dominé. It would be very useful to me."

She nodded and retrieved a DVD from a drawer. "I thought you might want it. Would you like to view it now?"

"Please."

She opened a slim laptop on her desk and slid the disk into the drive. When the video came up, she clicked on the timeline and the screen showed Valerie and Marcel standing as I'd first seen them, on the stairs outside the inner club.

The three vampires walked up the stairs and Marcel tried to stop them, saying they weren't members and he was under instruction to refuse entry. Valerie shrank back against the wall.

In a second, Marcel was shoved to one side by two of them, but I kept watching Valerie. Raul, the tall vampire, had her pressed against the wall. She was terrified and it looked to me as if that triggered a response from Raul. Her frantic blows against his body were ignored and died away as he fastened on her neck. Her face was tilted up and showed she was still aware and still frightened out of her skin, but her hands hung down limply.

"What the fuck are you doing?" shouted Rodrigo.

Whatever it was that set Raul off seemed to communicate itself to the third one, Antonio. He joined Raul.

Rodrigo had Marcel by a grip around his throat. He swore again and turned back to Marcel as his struggles were weakening. He glared at his face and then just simply let him go. Marcel slid down the wall. He didn't seem unconscious. He looked completely bewildered.

In the space of a few seconds of security video, the implications of the power of vampires sank in. Not just strong and fast, but capable of attacking a person's mind as well. No wonder they managed to stay hidden.

On screen, Rodrigo tore the other two off Valerie. He seemed exceptionally strong. Raul fought back and Rodrigo sent him slamming against the wall with a push.

They were shouting at each other, their voices distorted in the pickup. I didn't recognize the language.

It lasted only a minute. Rodrigo drove them out, leaving Valerie and Marcel sitting looking blankly at each other.

Dominé clicked on the player and the screen blanked.

In the silence, I retrieved a scrap of paper from my clutch bag. It was a bit torn off the club's check ticket for my cloak. Just enough. I wrote my cell number and name on it.

"Please give that to Marcel, and tell him to call me if he's worried."

She inclined her head.

I licked my lips. "And as a favor, would you erase the copies of that footage?"

"A favor for whom?" She watched me calmly as I struggled with what I could say that might convince her.

"For Valerie. I can't tell you why."

"Anything else?"

"Is there any way that she can be tracked from here — employee records, phone numbers?"

"Of course. You wish me to erase everything?"

"Just the contact information. And what about friends of hers?"

"You are very thorough in your requirements, Amber. I don't believe any of her friends would give her away."

"I wasn't thinking of a voluntary disclosure," I said.

"I see." She put the DVD in a case and handed it to me. "Then as far as I know, the only record of her address will be in my head. That, unfortunately, I cannot erase."

"Can I recommend precautions?" I said. "Some professional bodyguards to supplement the bouncers."

"These bodyguards, they will keep the three men away?"

"I think so." Even if they were going half crazy, they'd have to understand that forcing their way in here would bring the police after them. They couldn't wipe everyone's mind.

"Then surely I do not need to erase records?" asked Dominé.

"I would advise—"

"It seems," she said slowly, interrupting me, "I have many people to watch out for, on behalf of Valerie. This is not just about those men returning, is it?"

"No," I said. "But they're the most dangerous. The only protection you have is they want to operate in secret. They can't risk attracting too much notice. That alone should keep them from making trouble here, but not from pursuing Valerie if they realize that she is a security breach that they have to stop."

Dominé didn't say anything immediately, but ushered me away from the desk to an easy chair in a breakout area she had set up. I sat down stiffly.

"And the others who may come asking?" She opened a cabinet as I struggled against my conscience. "Well?" She turned and handed me a glass of wine. She turned the main lights off and sat opposite me, across a glass coffee table. The only light source was a low lamp shining onto the tabletop, leaving our faces in partial darkness.

"I can't say. I know I'm asking a lot here. If representatives of a government or federal institution..." I paused, unwilling to go on. I couldn't stand the thought of Valerie disappearing into the Obs laboratory through no fault of her own, but I was on the point of disobeying an army order.

Dominé held up a hand. "Enough," she said. "You demand a great deal from me, on trust."

"Yes." There seemed no other answer.

"And, in return, do you trust me?" She reached forward to pick up her wine. I'd thought she might be forty earlier in the night. Maybe it was the lighting, maybe she was tired, but she looked older now. Her eyes glittered in the gloom.

I tried to concentrate, sift through the night's jumble of emotions and images in my head. "Yes," I said again, and I meant it.

"*Vraiment*," she murmured, getting up to fetch something from a drawer in her desk.

She placed it on the table between us with a metallic click. It was one of the spiked collars her wait staff wore. My mouth went dry.

She sat back in the shadows, her fingers meditatively tracing the contours of the collar, sliding carefully over the barbs.

"Do you know, the *angoisse* was designed to teach young ladies the benefits of sitting straight and keeping the head upright?"

"Seems extreme," I managed to say.

"For that, it is, without doubt. Yet it outlasted the society and the thinking that designed it. And still, it has the capacity to teach." Her voice had become low, hypnotic. "I use it only as a gift. It may surprise you, Amber, but many come to me, thinking they wish to learn. Very few become *torquate* and wear the *angoisse*."

"I'm not interested."

"Quite. One is enough."

"What do you mean?"

"I mean you wear one already." She stirred. "You are wrapped in barbs so you cannot move. You can barely breathe without the pressure of them threatening to pierce your skin. Who has done this to you, Amber?"

The sounds of the club drifted in through all the soundproofing around her office. Much louder, my heart thudded in my ears. "I don't know what you mean," I said.

"I have been many years in my trade. A person who passes by might say I trade in pain. A person who lingers might say I trade in desire. I do neither. I simply enable people to look within themselves. And in return, I am granted some sight there."

Her description of my life now, wrapped around with threats from the prions in my blood, threats from the army, the pain of not being able to confide, it all seemed so accurate and yet how could she know any of this? How could she claim to see as much as she did? I had to believe in vampires. But what else was out there? Or rather, right here?

"Come," she said, picking up the *angoisse* and standing. "Trust me. I will show you, just briefly."

"Why?"

"You have helped one of mine. You have gifted me knowledge. This is my gift in return to you."

She walked behind me. My breath stuck in my throat. I held up a hand to stop her.

"It is a matter of trust, Amber."

I owed her for her trust. What was she going to do? Put something uncomfortable on my neck for a few seconds. How bad could it be? What would it feel like? My hand dropped.

I shivered as the metal scratched my neck. There was a click as she fastened it at the back and then her hands rested on my shoulders.

It was lighter than I'd thought. Barbs seemed to touch me everywhere, but nothing pierced me. I stayed very still, very upright, my chin up, and tried to breathe smoothly. I felt an obscure sense of pride. I could wear this if I had to. Seconds stretched. I flexed my neck slightly. I felt the barbs press into the skin. I raised my chin. Different barbs dug into different parts of my throat. How right she was. This was exactly how it felt.

With a twist, she undid the clasp and removed the collar.

"Familiar?" she said, returning to her seat and leaving the *angoisse* on the table.

My fingers passed over my neck, feeling the phantom pressure of the barbs and the old memories of fangs biting. I shivered again.

"The deepest lesson, that few really wish to learn," she said, "is that when that special desire comes, that overwhelming desire that will not be denied, the *angoisse* will not stop you doing what you truly wish. Whatever the cost."

We drained our wine and walked to the door.

"Whatever gods look down on you, Amber," she murmured, as if in prayer, "may they guide your steps, and your hand."

Chapter 10

Back at my apartment, the whole day seemed to recede into a dream.

The colonel had organized a data library on the internet. I accessed it from my laptop and started to upload the security footage from the club. The connection was lousy and I distracted myself by trying to write a report of what had happened. I was bone tired and my mind was fuzzy. In the end I kept it to a link to the footage and one word—*call*.

Lying back on my bed, waiting for the upload to complete, I reached out and picked up Tara's plaque from the bedside table.

Tara was my twin sister. She'd been stillborn. No one understood why I kept her plaque with me, or why I'd had it made, back when I was still at school.

People who lost loved ones sometimes had a photograph. I'd seen ones with birth and death dates on them. Tara had none of these. She'd never really been born, or died. There were no dates. There was no photograph. Others had tried to make out that she didn't exist because of that. Maybe I was the only person who still thought of her.

I held her plaque. It was so glossy that I could see myself in the reflection. I didn't need a photograph. This is what she would look like now.

"Tough day?" she said.

"You could say. Found the vampires though."

"Tell me about it."

It seemed easier to tell her than it had been to write a report. Of course, there were things I'd wanted to downplay in the report that I could just say to my twin.

"If there's a chance those three vampires were involved in the murder, then it's going to have to fall under the colonel's jurisdiction. How are you going to handle that with the police?"

"I don't know, at the moment. That's got to be something the army will have to handle. But will I be able to stay in the PD afterwards? That's another concern. The army won't keep finding me jobs, and if they stop doing that, how am I going to argue against going back to base?"

"So vampires can alter people's memories," she said. *"Cool. That would be a real neat trick to be able to do."*

I could hear her unspoken comment—it might not be so bad being a vampire if there were benefits like that.

"I don't want to become a vampire, Tara. I don't want to end up back in that cell."

"That's if the army could find you... When they can't even find vampires without your help."

I frowned. That was one way to think of it.

"But the footage shows vampires lose control sometimes. Is that what's in store for me?"

"Why would you think you would lose control like that?"

I lay back and tried to evaluate that objectively, but Tara wasn't finished.

"And hiding details about Valerie for her safety? Nothing to do with the fact that she's the one person you've met who can point at you and say 'vampire'?"

Sure, getting Valerie back to Nebraska and hiding her location was for her safety. But I couldn't lie to my twin. Tara was right; I'd actively moved to hide Valerie from the army, and the reasons were complicated.

I refused to follow that line of thought. I wasn't a vampire. I wasn't becoming a vampire. I just didn't want to risk Valerie confusing the issue with the army. There'd be some way for me to stay out of the Obs cell and live here in Denver.

I fell asleep telling myself that.

Chapter 11

SATURDAY

Fangs, just outside of my view, poised around my throat, pressing, gradually changing into the cold, metallic embrace of the *angoisse*. The taste of blood in my mouth. My cell phone woke me from another nightmare.

I knew who it had to be, and that was better than icy water in my face.

"Morning, Colonel." I tried to sound as if I'd been up for hours, as opposed to asleep for three.

"Sergeant."

"That lead on Club Agonia was good."

"That security video is from the club?" I could hear the tension in his voice—and maybe some subdued excitement. If I'd started to doubt myself, he had to be several steps beyond doubt. And now, suddenly, there was evidence.

"Yeah, but the vamps aren't a club thing. The club's just a sex club with the accent on kinky. There weren't any real vampires there at the Blood Orchid last night. Those three guys were visitors earlier this week. They're the real thing."

"How do you know? Did you make a positive ID? The video looks right, but it could be faked."

Knowing that this would put wheels in motion made me hesitate, but I couldn't duck the question.

"I didn't meet the vamps. I spoke to the girl. I could still smell them on her. And that was before I saw the video."

The colonel hesitated too. I could imagine the thoughts going through his head. How much could he trust me, or my sense of smell? What if I was wrong? Maybe he was even concerned how it would look on his record, not that he'd ever given that impression when we were both in Ops 4-10. But he was in the same position I was. He had to take it seriously. This was the whole reason for the Obs unit—find out if vampires exist in the US and then assess the threat.

"Where is the girl now?" he said.

I swallowed. "I'm not sure, sir. She's not at the club anymore from what I understand. Worked there under a false name." Right up to that point, I hadn't known which way I would go. I'd just stepped across a major line in my mind. The gap between my present self and the old Ops 4-10 Sergeant Farrell widened into a ravine.

How the hell did I think I was going to get away with hiding Valerie from Obs?

"Do you know where these three are then?" He was concentrating on practical matters.

"No, sir. There may have been a sighting of them in the vicinity of a murder later on Thursday evening. That murder's also raised a flag in my mind, but I haven't had time—"

"Is the murder connected to the club?"

"I don't know, sir. The neck wounds looked right, but I didn't get any time to check. As a rookie in patrol, I can't ask questions without people wondering why I'm trying to get involved. Even the little I've asked has caused some problems. I'd need to have access to someone senior cleared by you."

He was silent for a moment.

"I'll put together a squad," he said finally. "We'll be there by early afternoon Monday."

"Colonel, we know they must normally make a lot of effort to remain hidden. That video shows one or maybe two of them losing control, big time. What if that's a problem that escalates? Three of them go rogue in downtown

Denver? I know we don't have a specific location yet, but, with respect, sir, I think we need a rapid reaction force here today. And we need to figure out how to coordinate with the Denver PD."

"I hear you, Sergeant. First off, I have to remind you, I no longer control 4-10. I've got channels to go through."

I couldn't believe my ears. The colonel had to requisition troops?

"If we need to discuss this with the police when we arrive, we have a list of possible contacts in the PD to go to. It's got to be someone senior enough to keep it under wraps, but not so senior that they're political. One person. What we can't do is start spreading the knowledge around."

"Uh. Okay," I said. He hadn't asked for my input, but I was the one on the scene. "I'd recommend Lieutenant Morales. He's tipped to make Captain of Major Crimes soon. He's good."

"I'll take that on board," he said. "And Sergeant?"

"Yes sir?"

"Calling me sir is something you tend to do when you're really stressed. I need you operating clearly and efficiently." He paused to let that sink in. "Get a lead on those three before we show up and maybe we can keep this out of the police altogether."

The line went dead.

Shit.

He was right. Ops 4-10 wasn't a unit where you used 'sir' a lot. On ops, we hadn't even used ranks. But how exactly did he expect me not to be stressed? I was allowed out of the Obs cell on the basis I didn't turn, didn't leak, supported myself and did the jobs the army threw at me. If I did the job and identified vampires in the US, I made myself redundant, or the police threw me out, or I got classified as a vampire anyway. Or all three. Every route seemed to point back to the Obs cell.

I wasn't going back there willingly, whatever happened. And I wasn't going to send anyone like Valerie there on just the suspicion they might turn.

That was all to worry about later. The three vampires had to be caught. First step, I had to find a lead.

Guess I'd have to skip the repair of the fuel pump on my car and head downtown instead.

Shit again.

My car decided that wasn't a good plan. I made it to Rom's garage at midmorning, only thanks to his tow truck.

I already had the new fuel pump, and the cost of hiring Rom's car bay and tools was nothing compared to getting a garage to fix it, even after the cost of having it towed here.

The reason for that cost, however, was the job was a stone bitch. The fuel pump lived in the fuel tank, so everything had to be taken off and then reassembled.

Rom grinned and dived back under the hood of his current job, a BMW.

I pulled on my coveralls and got on with it.

After half an hour, Jo came in, wearing old clothes, and helped. Balancing the time spent answering her questions and the instructions I had to give her against how much time I saved doing the job myself was a close thing, but we spent half the time laughing. Jo couldn't have realized it, but it was exactly the distraction I needed.

Rom came and helped with the last part when Jo had to leave.

Afterwards, I let the engine run while I cleaned up.

Rom was leaning against my car, wiping his hands while he listened to the steady idle. I'd kept my shirt on, but he hadn't. My eyes roved. He wasn't my dream man, by any stretch, but he had pretty ripply bits when he moved around, and that dark wavy hair went so well with the gypsy brown eyes.

I sighed. The colonel would spontaneously implode if I somehow infected anyone else with prions, and his medical team wouldn't rule out what they tactfully called 'intimate contact' as a method for infecting other people. So, the rules said no touch. But they didn't say no look.

"Work out okay at Agonia?" he asked when I rejoined him.

"Yeah." I rolled the coveralls into a plastic bag and tossed it in the trunk.

"It really not for fun?"

"Not for fun at all. Apart from my entrance, thanks to you." I reached into the car and blipped the gas pedal. The engine revved up with no hesitation. Woo hoo.

He shrugged off the compliment. "You a PI?"

Rom didn't speak too well, but that didn't affect my judgment on his brain, and yeah, what I was doing for the colonel was closer to a sort of exotic PI job than police work. Except maybe the undercover stuff the DEA did. Allegedly.

"Yeah, something like that. Some of the time."

Rom got the hint and backed off from asking about my work. I didn't want people to know I was in the police. Not for any feelings on my part, but I didn't want people reacting differently to me.

He stuck his hands deep into his pockets and eased his weight from one foot to the other.

"This been good for Jofranka," he said finally. "She needs something to help her feel okay about herself. Strong. Smart. You know?"

I nodded. Helping people find their potential was something I enjoyed and I knew he was asking about that in his roundabout sort of way. Jo didn't need a lot, she had a quick mind and a thirst to try things. But I could hardly recommend myself as a mentor—or friend. Not with the doubts hanging over me.

"I'll think it over," I said. "I'll keep an eye open."

I'd heard my cell ring a couple of times while I was working and I picked it up now to check who'd called. The number surprised me; it was a guy called Greg Whitman who I'd worked with at my last job.

I walked out of the garage to call him back.

When I'd managed to get out of the army's laboratory, they'd recommended a safe, steady job. Some high watt light bulb decided that meant accounting. I was in no position to argue, and if spreadsheets and learning financial regulations was my ticket out, I was going to take it. The big thing going for it was they'd found me a position in a company here in my hometown of Denver.

It had worked out better than expected, right up until I blew the company apart by exposing the criminal behavior of the CEO. In the resulting chaos, Whitman had taken the best of the staff and the best of the clients and set up on his own. You could say I'd helped him, but I wasn't expecting any calls from him, and I wasn't going back to being a trainee accountant or bookkeeper.

"Amber! Thanks for calling back. How are you?"

"I'm good, thanks. I heard your new company is going great. Congratulations."

"Ah, thanks. Look, Amber, I don't want to take up too much of your time on the weekend. I'm due at the golf club in a few minutes, but do you think you could make time to come in on Monday and have a talk?"

"What about?"

"Well, y'know, what you did impressed me, I'll say that. And it impressed a lot of the old clients, too. Turns out, there may be a business in there for you."

"I don't follow, Mr. Whitman. What kind of a business are you talking about?"

"Private investigations for commercial clients. I know," he hurried on, "PIs are a dime a dozen, but listen to me, the clients need someone who understands financial information."

"I don't know, I have a job. I'm a policewoman."

"Yeah, and cops are great. Look, give it some thought over the weekend and call me Monday. We can talk it through. Gotta go now. Talk Monday. Okay?"

"Okay."

I ended the call, and briefly indulged in a fantasy of running my own little PI business, before squashing it. Whatever he said about commercial clients, PIs make their steady income staking out lap dancing joints in divorce cases. I'd call and turn it down on Monday. Anyway, the colonel would go ape-shit if I tried to pull something like that.

No, I needed to take police work more seriously, stop daydreaming, stop shooting my mouth off, develop respect for the positions of authority, the rank and not the person, yadda, yadda, how hard could all that be? I did it in the army. Except then, I really had been a rookie. Now I had more experience in crisis situations than half the Denver PD put together, and I still didn't get the respect I'd had in Ops 4-10.

The opportunity to spend some time trying to find a lead had gone when my car refused to start this morning. I only had an hour or so before I needed to show up for the Saturday night shift on patrol. I would have to try again tomorrow.

Meantime, I had a session booked I didn't want to miss. I'd laughed some of my frustrations away with Jo earlier, now maybe I could burn the rest of them out.

Chapter 12

"You are focusing too much on me," Liu said. "Loosen your mind, perceive everything."

I snorted. "Last time, Shi Fu, you were telling me to focus on your eyes."

"And in contemplation of the contradiction, your mind will approach the ideal."

Liu didn't smile much, but I had a feel for his sense of humor. Our one minute breather over, we lifted the padded gloves and closed again.

I took great care when I sparred with his other students. On top of ten years studying martial arts, my strength and speed had increased since I was bitten. I didn't want to break someone's jaw accidentally.

This was not a concern with Liu. Despite being older than me, he was startlingly quick and elusive. I got a real thrill out of landing more than a couple of blows on him in a sparring session like this one, where we were essentially boxing, limiting ourselves to punches.

It focused me. It helped force me to put everything else aside and concentrate on hitting that weaving target without picking up too many hits myself. That would be good at the moment—I could come back fresh to the problems of what to do before the colonel arrived on Monday.

Liu enjoyed it as well, usually.

He called an end after the next flurry of blocks and jabs. We'd worked up a sweat, but I had expected a couple more rounds.

"Come," he said, stripping his gloves and head protector off. He walked to the corner of the Kwan. "Follow me in the form."

He started to move through one of the standard forms. My body hitched onto the muscle memory and I flowed along with him without having to think about it.

"Good," he said. "The body is engaged. The small mind is engaged. The large mind can roam free." He sank into an asymmetric stretch. "And you can tell me what is bothering you."

"Huh?" I missed a move and had to catch up.

"You're never fully absorbed in the moment, Amber," he said, spinning on the spot and blocking attacks from imaginary assailants. "You always hold a little back. But today, you are holding a lot back. Why?"

We stepped back in sync. "I'm bothered by things at work."

"This is seldom so. What bothers people may be rooted in work or fed at work, but more often it is simply that it remains unresolved in the time spent at work." He crouched and came up smoothly on one leg, held it perfectly still. "What is work?"

I wobbled a bit, thrown by the question. "Everything I do when I'm in uniform."

"So all the rest is play."

I didn't talk to anyone, other than the colonel, about what I did for the army. I was living two lives and there was a sense of inevitability that they would cross. I'd dealt with stress and secrecy in Ops 4-10, but I'd had support from people in the same position. Here, I was alone. I had no one I could truly share with, let alone receive support from. Sure, I had help from the PD. Help appropriate for a rookie doing her job.

There wasn't any play. It had all but disappeared into the colonel's work, exercise, eating and sleeping. I didn't want to lie to Liu.

My balance went to hell, and I had to bring my foot down and move into the next sequence of moves early. Damn. I came here to stop thinking about these things.

He sighed.

"Sit," he said, folding down into a half lotus. I copied him.

There was a small class doing exercises at the other end of the Kwan, leaving us alone.

"I enjoy you attending this Kwan," he said and paused. "But I am worried for you."

"Shi Fu?"

"Your training in the army has given you such control. The Western world calls this 'iron control.' You use this to completely hide things deep inside." He held up a hand to stop me from interrupting. "But iron can rust. Iron can become brittle. There are angers and forces buried in you that will find their way out. If they do this by themselves they can destroy you."

Liu could sound obscure at times, but we'd never had a conversation like this before. With anyone else, it would have just been embarrassing. But Liu seemed to be talking to something inside me that was taking note.

"Whatever it is, you cannot continue to do what you are doing," he said. "You must change. You will change; you have no option except how much you are in control of the change."

Well, what would he advise, if I told him everything that was happening?

Even thinking about it at a mundane level: should I become a PI? Cut myself off from what little support the police were able to provide me? At least then, I wouldn't be keeping things from them.

"Everywhere you hide your true self, you do damage, to yourself and to those you are hiding from."

Would he say I should stop seeing my family?

Liu watched me mull through what he'd said.

"If you wish, we will talk again, after sessions."

I nodded silently.

"For now, trust to your instincts more. Trust them against the rote learning that tells you that things must be so. You are more powerful than you think, if you let yourself be."

He rose suddenly. "Now, more sparring," he said.

"Boxing again?" I put my gloves back on, but he shook his head.

"Jujitsu, I think. Not with me. With Tullah."

"Who?"

"Me."

I turned to look and sighed. I was going to have to go back to being careful again. Tullah was shorter and slighter than me, and she looked as if she was still in college. She was some exotic blend of Chinese, but martial arts aren't braided into the genome, they have to be learned. Liu sometimes had me sparring against students who thought they had come a long way. A sort of salutary lesson against getting big-headed.

If she read my thoughts, she made no sign of it. Her face, partly covered by the head protector, was shiny and open. She moved well at least.

We squared off on the mats and I made a standard lunge. A feint, to see how quickly she got out of the way.

She didn't jerk back, she didn't move away. She moved in. Inside the span of my arms, she canceled any advantage of reach I had. My weight was too far forward, my center of gravity higher than hers, and she grabbed the collar of my *gi*, crouched and twisted herself, so that my momentum made me fall over her. Then she heaved and I was tossed in the air.

Luckily, all the necessary reactions had been burned into me. I tucked up and rolled right back onto my feet, coming back up ready for a secondary attack. Purely as a matter of form.

It was a good thing that kind of action had been drilled into me. Tullah was right in there, pressing home her attack.

Instincts took over and I caught her coming in off balance against my stable stance. I thumped her in the belly and then threw her over my hip.

She rolled neatly and bounced back onto her feet, just like I had, ready in case I was already coming in. I wasn't. I was standing there berating myself for being an overconfident asshole.

"That was *awesome!*" she squealed. And came straight back at me.

Ten minutes later we were both dripping in sweat, and I'd been infected with her laughter.

But I had a date with Officer Knight, so I reluctantly put up my gloves in surrender.

She tossed her head protector aside and gave me a hug.

"Thank you so much, Amber. I can call you Amber, can't I? I've seen you practicing but Pa didn't want me to spar with you. I've had to go on at him for, like, *ages*."

"Whoa! Master Liu is your dad?"

"Yeah. He's pretty cool."

"Okay." I guessed I would call him pretty cool if I was nineteen years old and overfilled with exuberance.

"When are you coming back? Can we spar again?"

"Yeah, yeah, of course. Tuesday probably. I won't go so easy on you next time," I said.

Ha!

"Awesome."

I had a sudden thought. "And what if I sent someone to train with you? She might have a problem persuading her parents or her uncle to pay for coaching, but if she could just join in and see what it's like? Ask a few questions?" I said, innocently.

"Yeah, sure."

"Her name's Jo. I'll send you her cell."

"Okay. Thanks so much for today." She skipped away.

I grinned. *Oh, that was evil.* But they'd wear each other out instead of me.

I waved goodbye to Liu and went to shower.

It didn't escape me that he'd matched me up with Tullah deliberately and given me a message in one neat maneuver.

His earlier comments were replaying in my mind. Could he really see things inside me?

What if his message was about things going on deeper inside me? What if he was saying I'd be better off not fighting it, just becoming a vampire? Disappear into their world. All this crap would just go away then. Life would be simpler.

What would it feel like, being a vampire?

I shut that thought down. Anyway, there was no way he could see stuff like that inside me.

Even at a surface level, he had certainly given me lots to think about, but Saturday night on patrol wasn't going to be the place for it.

Chapter 13

Saturday's patrol with Knight was like any other Saturday—the constant feel that things could become a riot with the wrong spark. The feeling of disbelief when they didn't.

I wasn't sure whether he'd worked through his anger, or he was just giving me another chance, but Knight acted as if the last shift hadn't happened.

He was on good form with his patter as we went from incident to incident. I heard things I hadn't heard before. Some of them were useful.

We were making our way back after a trip to the station to hand over an incompetent burglar, stoned out of his mind, when I turned onto 12th and an idea formed about checking out Werner Schumacher's sighting on Friday night.

"Y'know, it used to be that burglars were worth chasing," Knight was saying. "They were professionals. It gave you a sense of achievement to bring them in. Now the guy doesn't even notice us walking up behind him."

"I don't think he even knew we were at the station," I said. "It'll be fun for him when he wakes up in the morning." We drew level with the alley where the body had been found and I let the car slow. The traffic was light.

"It's quieter," I said.

"Yeah, well, learn to enjoy it," he said. "That might help keep you alert. Better than bored, careless and dead."

I nodded in time with the emphasis he beat out on the dash. I'd learned that lesson in harder schools than he had, where the gap between careless and dead was frighteningly small. Still, it was sound advice, the sort of thing a rookie would need to hear.

We passed the Schumachers' shop. Werner had looked out and seen three men walking along here. From his description, the security camera I'd seen from the club, and the death of the man whose body we'd found in the dumpster, it was a reasonable assumption that they were the same group.

I didn't have proof and I couldn't talk it through with Knight, but we were in the right place and I could use the time to think about it.

They'd walked along here. They'd been wearing coats. Of course, they could have parked a car and walked the last bit. If they did that, how had they picked their parking spot? Why not park right outside where they were going? If they didn't want the car to be seen where they were going, how far would they walk? Where would they park that would make them feel it was safe?

"What's up?" asked Knight, finally.

"I'm practicing being a detective," I said. He knew which case I was talking about. "I heard that they've identified the vic and he shared an apartment backing onto the alley. I'm guessing he was dumped so his roommates didn't find him. The body might never have been found, or only found when it went to the dump."

"You know what Buchanan will think about you getting involved?"

"Humor me. Buchanan's not in the car with us. We're just kicking it around."

"Yeah? Okay, so he still wasn't killed in the apartment or the alley. He had to have bled out someplace else. Where? How did they get him back there?"

I knew an answer to that—he'd been bled out right in that apartment, but I wasn't about to share how that was.

"Not relevant at the moment," I said instead. "My point is, the three guys we have reported walking here at the right time are either suspects or need to be questioned."

Knight played along with it, but I could tell what he thought about the rookie trying to be detective.

"So," I said. "Three guys in coats. Where did they walk from?"

He waved his hands. "There are buses, there are roads going everywhere. There's the path along the creek. They could have come from anywhere."

"Yeah, but why park up at the stadium, say, and walk down here to commit a murder? You wouldn't walk miles. You wouldn't take a bus or a taxi and leave a trail. Not three guys together. Gut feel says they came by car, but they didn't want to park right by the apartment."

"Okay, fair enough, but where does that get you?"

"Well, they live here, or work here, or have someplace to park that doesn't raise suspicions. Someplace private, where they're not going to be noticed or need to buy a ticket."

"Like a private garage?"

"Or a business they work at."

Knight shook his head. "They wouldn't feel safe. Some other employee might come in and see the car." He frowned. "Unless it was a small, three-man business."

He made a fair point. I nodded.

We'd gone as far as Speer Boulevard. Speer cuts diagonally northwest to southeast. It's a major road, split into north and southbound lanes by Cherry Creek and the trail. It felt like a border. Past it were school sports fields, businesses and a park. It didn't feel right, them coming that far, so I turned and drove slowly back, looking at the side roads.

One of these?

"It's all kinds of problem, this case," Knight said.

"Why especially?"

"Press. Most murders, however they get reported, people read the details and they know, or think they know, why the person was killed. They move on, they say they're not like that, it's not going to happen to them." Knight shrugged. "But this one is strange, especially when you add in the thing about the blood. If the press gets hold of that before we've caught the perps and explained it all away, they blow it up. 'Police don't even know where the murder was committed'—you know the kind of story. Things like that make people feel unsafe. It gets air time. It makes everyone look bad. The mayor gets unhappy, the chief gets it in the ear and we get it in the neck."

I snorted. I was looking down the side streets hoping for inspiration to strike.

Is this the sort of place vampires hang out?

"What makes the brass happy are murders that can be pigeonholed in one of the known categories," Knight said, counting things on his fingers. "Gangs killing each other, mugging gone bad in the wrong part of town, crime of passion, revenge, that sort of thing. What they don't want to hear is anything that makes Joe Average feel unsafe. Psychopaths, serial killers, murders the police don't understand, and so on."

Vampires, I thought.

Knight ran his hand over his face. "Look, you did okay Friday night." He sighed. "It's kinda difficult remembering you're not a rookie like the others."

I nodded.

"Word is," he went on, "your scores are good enough for the SWAT team."

"Thanks." That wouldn't be so bad. Not one partner, but a team. Much more like the army. But I'd need to do my time on patrol first, and for that I needed a partner like Knight.

"But if you want my advice, which is free, and you get it anyway..."

I managed a sickly grin. "Hit me."

"Instructor."

"Oh, come on!"

"I have only one more thing to say about it. Something very important." He waited till he saw he had my attention. "Regular hours." He tapped the clock on the dash, and we laughed.

Then he turned serious again. "Farrell, listen to me, just this once, hey? This one is the kind of case you want to keep as far away from as you can," he said. "Don't do anything you aren't specifically told to do. Don't start spouting any theories."

Yeah. Unfortunately, not an option.

The buildings on the right, down Cheyenne Street, looked like an interesting mix, but it was one-way. Further up, near the Schumachers', I was thinking about doing the circuit and driving back up Cheyenne when I saw a group of girls on the street. They looked far too young to be out this late.

"Whoa," I said. "How old are those kids? No way their parents let them out at this time of night." I stopped the car. "And if they did, they shouldn't have." Especially if there were vampires roaming the neighborhood. I shivered at the thought of those guys on the video getting hold of a kid.

"Sneaked out, probably. Not really our problem," Knight said, but he got out with me. They were even younger up close. Young enough so that the approach of 'authority'—namely me in my scary police uniform—evaporated all the bravado of being out on the streets at night. The group was too young to know what to do or where to go. They wouldn't get into any bars. The whole purpose seemed to have been to put on makeup and hang out with their friends without their parents knowing.

Fine, but not in this neighborhood, and not this late. Not on my watch.

"Evening, girls." Knight beat me to it, sounding a little awkward. "I don't think this is an appropriate place for you to be at this time." He pointed at one in the front. "Where's your home?"

The girls had regained a little courage and were just about to start some bluffing and back-talk, when I recognized a face at the back, even with the Goth makeup.

"Emily Schumacher, isn't it?" I reached through the group and got her shoulder. Her friends eased away as if I'd just told them she had the plague.

"Err...yeah," she admitted.

Her look was mirrored on every face. *Aw crap, busted.*

Immediately followed by thoughts of what their parents were going to do. It was almost funny.

Knight and I shepherded them a couple of blocks, to where the Schumachers lived. Werner came running out as we arrived. He'd just discovered Emily missing.

The Schumachers handled it well. I could see they were upset, but there was no shouting. Klara recognized the girls and had them sit in the kitchen while she started calling their parents. She was merciful enough to bring out some wipes so they could clean up before being seen. Poor Emily wouldn't have that advantage.

Werner wiped the sweat off his brow, thanked us several times and checked that there wasn't anything more going to come of it.

We assured Werner it wasn't a problem and walked back to the car.

Now, where was I? A circuit to come back up Cheyenne. But Knight had gotten bored.

"Take a left here and head up to the center," he said. "We haven't been up that end yet tonight."

We hadn't, and there just happened to be an all-night café with good donuts that way. I sighed. He was my partner and I was the rookie. I turned left.

We handed things over to the graveyard shift, making it feel like an early night for us. A few minutes later, and we'd have caught the radio calls about the next murder, the one that moved it all a huge step closer to me.

Chapter 14

SUNDAY

I spent the morning down at the station, looking at traffic footage for the cameras in the vicinity of the first murder and cross checking with the area around Club Agonia. It's not the quick and easy job they show on TV, not by a long way.

Lunch was at Mom's. It wasn't a success. Naturally, she always wanted to know what was going on in my life and there was almost nothing I could tell her. It frustrated me and it hurt her. I escaped as soon as I could and went back to trying to figure out where the vampires had come from and what cars they drove.

In the late afternoon, I took a break and stopped in at the Schumachers.

We sat in their living room. Klara brought out some little Bavarian cakes and cookies that were a regional specialty. The treats tempted Emily downstairs.

Not surprisingly, she wasn't made up today. I gathered the makeup had been restricted to pre-agreed get-togethers, and only one per week was going to be allowed, which had to be supervised. The rest of the time, she was completely grounded. She was only allowed out for school or with her parents.

It probably seemed fairer to me than it did to her.

What did surprise me was she didn't hold a grudge. She wasn't my best friend, but she didn't sit there glaring at me. I really liked that.

Klara got me to talk a little about myself, and Emily's curiosity fought against her attempt to be cool and distant.

She seemed interested in the little stories I told about what I'd done in the police, and stuff from my days at South High. I left out everything from the army and all that led up to it.

Werner asked what I did on my days off, and rather than stonewalling, I said I went clubbing, making out it was my choice and not part of my duties, checking for vampires.

Stroke of genius. The real breakthrough came when I mentioned a particular dance club I'd been to a month before. The club was radical, apparently. The coolest place on earth. Emily was as deeply impressed as someone who has only experienced the club second or third hand could be. She went through a list of people she said had gone there and they were all, like, really, really cool too. I doubt she actually knew any of them.

Finally she stopped. "But you don't look…" she hesitated.

"Like a Goth?" I said. I tried to tiptoe here. Tact is not my strong suit. "Or just a person with any sense of style?"

Emily tensed up.

"Emily, some people take a style and let it define them. Well, it's a free world. The rest of us, we can take the style and use it. And then the next day, maybe we'll try a different one. There were things I wore fifteen years ago which would make you laugh. But you would have worn them, back then."

She thought about that a bit. "Do you dress up then?"

Second stroke of genius, sort of. I'd taken photos of myself in full vampire dress on my cell phone just before I'd gone off to Club Agonia. My own personal record of the things I had to do. I got out my cell, and pulled the pictures up.

Emily pounced, and before I could stop her, she had shown Klara and Werner. Fortunately, they saw the funny side.

When I left half an hour later, Emily begged me to come back next time her friends were around, and never, ever to delete those way cool photos.

Chapter 15

At roll call for the graveyard shift, there was no sign of Knight.

The other crews were talking about yesterday's murder. I was confused about when that was by the hours I had been keeping. I thought they were talking about the body I'd found. They weren't. Finally it sank in that they were talking about a dead man that had shown up twelve hours ago, on yesterday's graveyard shift. With the same MO.

I wanted details, but we were interrupted by the duty sergeant, who read the notices and confirmed the crews. After that, the rest of them hurried off.

There was still no sign of Knight.

It wasn't that unusual to have to run a patrol single-handed when a colleague called in sick at the last minute, but nothing had been said.

I had just stuck my head around the door to ask the duty Sergeant, Bill Carver, when Knight appeared.

"Sorry, got held up," he said.

"Oh?"

I thought he wasn't going to say any more, but he did. "Homicide wanted to check some stuff about patrol."

I shrugged. I thought there were better ways to do that, but no one is interested in what the rookie has to say.

"Did you hear there was another body yesterday with the same MO?" I asked.

"Yeah."

"Where was it? Have they got a name?"

Knight stopped abruptly and grabbed my arm. "Look, Farrell, I don't want to talk about it, okay? Remember what I said about the murder the other night? This qualifies too. You don't want to talk about it either." His finger stabbed out at me for emphasis. "You don't want to get involved. You don't want to be seen scanning traffic cameras on some case that is not your concern. You got that, rookie?"

Okay.

What the hell had bitten his ass? My getting in trouble for sticking my nose into a case on my own wasn't going to reflect on him.

"I understand," I said.

I had to drop it. I was supposed to be on patrol for the next four hours, not solving cases. I'd pick it up afterwards.

This was routine, so we didn't need to talk any more while I got us out of the parking lot and onto our patrol area. There are points you visit repeatedly during a patrol and I started by cruising past the closest, working our way in a zigzag to the far end of our assigned precinct before starting the standard pattern.

Something was bothering me. I mentally ran down my list of things inside and outside work to check if I'd forgotten something. I came up blank. I was going to crack a joke about it being too quiet, when I realized that was exactly what was bothering me. Knight hadn't said a word since we got in. Surely it wasn't all about Friday? Maybe he had been chewed out for something I'd done.

"All okay?" I asked.

"Yeah." He lapsed back into silence, slumped down in the seat. If that was what talking with Homicide did to him, I'd advise skipping it next time.

"So, our last few graveyard shifts gets you two days off next weekend," I said. "Got any plans?"

"Chores. Then I'll catch the ball game," he said and sat up straighter. "I'll have some friends around, grill a few steaks, drink a few beers. What about you?"

At least that had got a couple of sentences from him. "I hadn't planned anything. Ball game sounds good."

"No friends coming around?"

We'd never met outside of work. We'd never spoken about what we did outside of work. I was at a difficult point here. Partners talked about things. I wanted to feel easy with Knight. On the other hand, I didn't want to have him invite me over or get the wrong idea.

"I haven't had time," I said.

"So, what do you do? Forget what you might get up to next weekend. We had a day off on Friday. You must have done something after you caught up on sleep?"

"I fixed my car," I said.

"The Focus? It's stopped bouncing?"

"Pretty much." The car had become the standing joke of the parking lot in the week since the fuel pump started to fail. Or rather, the jerking joke. A rich source of humor for the boys.

"You didn't spend all day doing that though. What else?"

Dressed up as a vampire and went hunting. What the hell do I say? And why the hell the sudden interest?

"Oh, I went out that night." I kept it vague, hoping he'd move on to something else. It was too early in the shift to divert him with donuts.

"Where?"

"Just a dance club. Why?"

Something was off. He'd had a session with Homicide and now he was asking me what I do during my time off? Who really wanted to know? And why?

"I don't know," he said, backing off. "We've never talked about it. I guess I've just realized I don't know what my partner gets up to, on her days off."

"Trust me, it's boring at the moment," I said. "All my old friends from school are gone or married, and my friends from the army are miles away. I've been so busy getting settled back in, I haven't really had time."

I hadn't missed that 'partner' he'd thrown in there, but what to make of it? Did he really mean he felt we were partners now, or was it a slip?

There was a call on the radio, and conversation ground to a halt. Between calls it limped along until we finally dropped it. A thick fog rolled in across the city and the number of calls dropped. But Knight didn't launch into his usual spiel at any time. Something was definitely wrong.

Chapter 16

MONDAY

Even for a foggy 4 a.m., it was quiet.

We'd returned to the station and parked the cruiser.

I needed to find out the details on the murder from last night. The colonel was arriving at midday, and I hadn't gotten a solid lead for him on the vampires. The best I could do was have all the related information ready.

I switched my cell on, dawdling behind Knight as he strode toward the door.

There were ten missed calls from Dominé, the last one ten minutes ago.

My stomach lurched. This couldn't be good. What had gone wrong?

She answered immediately, as if she'd been sitting by the phone.

"Amber, please, we need your help."

"What's happened?"

"Did you not hear? About Marcel?"

"No, I haven't heard anything about Marcel. Slow down, tell me what's going on."

"There's no time. The police have been here—"

"Hold it." I stopped her, the first hints of a sick certainty rising in my gorge. "Mike," I called to Knight, slipping into using his first name without thought. He stopped and waited while I caught up to him.

"What was the name of the guy killed last night? The one they thought was the same MO?"

He frowned. "Marc Ellis. Why?"

Shit.

"Can't stop now. I'll explain later." I sprinted towards my car.

Marc Ellis. Valery Hawks. Marcel and Valerie. Dominé's way of making everything sound more exotic.

"Amber," Knight called out behind me. "Wait! We have to talk. You can't hold out on your partner!"

Like he had, all this last patrol.

"Dominé?" I said.

"I'm here."

"Was his real name Marc Ellis?"

"Yes, yes, of course, I'm sorry, I forgot you wouldn't know."

I reached the car and slid inside. My mind was linking things up, but it was far too late.

Marcel the artist. Valerie the artist. They worked together at the club. She had paintings of his, in her folder.

"Marcel knew where Valerie lives?" I said as the car started.

"I don't know, Amber, truly, I don't, but I am afraid—"

"I couldn't get an answer from Valerie's home number," I said. "I thought that meant she'd gone."

"She's not in Nebraska," said Dominé. "I called her mother. I called her cell. I've left messages. There is nothing."

"Did you go to her apartment?"

"I tried the intercom outside but there was no response. No lights on in her apartment. That was the first time I called you."

"I'll be there in a few minutes. I'll call you back."

I ended the call and pulled out of the parking lot, my tires screeching. Knight had been walking towards me, trying to flag me down, but I couldn't stop. Wouldn't.

The lights were still off in Valerie's apartment. Given the time, that wasn't surprising. Everything was calm and orderly on the surface.

Except when I looked carefully, I could see the outside lock was damaged. It hadn't been last time. I drew my gun. Anger and frustration boiling over in me, I gave it a hard shove and I was through. I sprinted up the stairs.

I could smell vampire long before I got to her door.

It was locked.

"Valerie!" I pounded on the door until the second smell started to seep into my awareness. Then I took a couple of steps back and kicked right through it.

I flicked on the lights, hoping I was wrong. Anything, anything but what I found.

Pictures hung skew. One penguin painting looked up from the floor, the glass shattered and the frame splintered, the previously happy look distorted into bewilderment.

Leo the cat was against the wall in the hallway, looking like he'd been casually thrown aside. His back was broken.

Chairs in the living room were overturned. There'd been a brief, futile struggle.

Valerie was lying sprawled on her back in the living room, arms above her head and her throat savagely torn. Her clothes were twisted and ripped, as if she'd been held down and struggled wildly. Her face had frozen into a rictus of pain and despair. There was no wide pool of blood, and she was so pale.

I dropped to my knees beside her. Under my questing fingers, there was no pulse beneath her jaw. No life in the wide, shocked eyes.

There was blood and skin under her fingernails. She'd fought and scratched, but she'd trained her hands to paint, not to fight. She'd had no chance against one of them, let alone three.

Looking at her throat, I put my hand to my own. These were not the neat punctures I'd seen on the first victim. This was the kind of savagery I'd experienced in the jungles of South America. Were these vampires losing control?

A scrap of paper dropped on the floor caught my attention. I didn't need to pick it up to recognize it as the coat check I'd written my number on and asked Dominé to give to Marcel.

They'd gone looking. They hadn't found Valerie, so they'd found Marcel instead. And before they'd killed him, he'd given them Valerie's address.

My fingers were numb, fumbling with the radio button.

"Farrell here," I said, my voice strained. "I need Homicide."

Chapter 17

CSI and the ME were inside the apartment.

I'd left the station in my own car, so I didn't have crime scene forms or tape. I was improvising, standing in the doorway with a notebook. Mainly, I was working at not revisiting all the decisions I'd made over the last few days. They kept coming at me like a blurry nightmare.

I'd been awake for over twenty hours. I desperately wanted another patrol car to come spell me. Given the complications of my connection with this case, I would have thought there would have been someone here by now.

Instead of my relief, the next to arrive was Buchanan. He had a second detective in tow, an older guy I hadn't met before. Buchanan looked at my notepaper crime scene form as if I'd personally insulted him, but he signed. The second guy signed as Nunez, and stayed while Buchanan went into the living room to get in CSI's way.

"You called it in as the same MO?" Nunez asked.

"Yeah, from what I heard," I said. "Throat torn up. Not as much blood as expected."

"Was the body moved here?"

No. I shrugged the question away. "Ask CSI."

Nunez looked at the door. "Was it like this when you got here?" He pointed at the damage.

"No. I kicked it."

Just like that, we were on a slide to questions I couldn't answer without the colonel's say-so. If I said I'd smelled vampires, Nunez would call for restraints.

"Why?" Buchanan came back out to join the party.

I couldn't just stand here and refuse to answer questions.

"I believed the victim was in danger."

"How did you work that out, Farrell?" Buchanan eyed me coldly.

The anger he'd stoked so well last time came back to the surface, but I kept it in hand.

"The last victim, Marc Ellis, worked with her. There was an incident at their work prior to Ellis's murder that involved both of them. I received a call from her boss saying she'd hadn't gone home to Nebraska as expected. I dropped by and the main door downstairs was damaged. There was no response from inside the apartment and I thought I smelled something."

It sounded thin as tissue.

A couple of uniforms arrived at that point. I handed one of them my makeshift crime scene form and let them take over.

Buchanan and Nunez crowded me to one side.

"You're familiar with this victim?" Buchanan's tone was terse.

"Not really."

"You know where she lives, where she works, you know her travel plans, you know her friends…" Nunez said.

"I gave her a ride home once."

Nunez and Buchanan exchanged looks.

After a pause, Buchanan nodded. "You're with us," he said to me. "We'll need a statement down at the station."

"Okay, my car's outside," I said. I didn't want to end up back at the station without a car.

"Give me a lift," Buchanan said.

It wasn't a request.

I'd showed up out of nowhere, knew the victim well enough to decide to kick her door down and I discovered a murder that was linked to two more. Just those details were enough to make me a person of interest. Add the possibility of press speculation on top, and the pressure on Homicide would be mounting. They'd want a detailed statement from me and I wouldn't be able to tell them enough to satisfy them.

As we walked out to the cars, I felt a mounting anger at everything. Why couldn't the colonel have gotten here sooner? Why did this investigation have to land on Buchanan's desk? Why did I have to be the damn fuse point all the time?

Not helpful at the moment. I needed to be thinking clearly. I pushed the anger back down.

Buchanan slid into the passenger seat and I pulled out of the parking lot, Nunez following close behind us.

Buchanan let out a sigh and pinched the bridge of his nose. He hadn't gotten to bed either, by the look of it.

"You did okay," he said finally.

Huh? What the hell?

"Thanks," I replied cautiously.

"Knight said you lit out like your tail was on fire."

"There was a chance she was alive."

And my partner was reporting on me. Frigging fantastic. All those questions on patrol last night. Knight talks to Homicide and all of a sudden he's interested in what I did on Friday. Yeah.

Buchanan's shoulders slumped.

"We need more resources," he said. "You're half in anyway. We're going to need you to come on board. Who's in charge of your duty rosters?"

"Sergeant Carver." I was having trouble keeping up with him. He wanted me on his team? Yeah. My bullshit meter went into the red zone.

"Okay. I'll talk to him." He looked out the window. "The team needs to keep our story straight here. If we start talking about serial killers, the press will be all over us. It won't look good, and believe me, this case is being watched all the way to the top. If we screw it up, they'll know who to blame."

And so convenient for Detective Buchanan if he could redirect the blame downwards.

But I needed to get every last fact out of Buchanan for the colonel. The easiest way would be to pretend I was taken in by his invitation to join his team.

"You transferring me from patrol to your investigation team?"

"Yeah. We'll sort the details out later. You don't want to stay in patrol, do you? It'd be a waste."

"No, I don't want to stay in patrol," I said.

But I don't believe your bullshit that you can shift me around just like that. Or that you've suddenly realized I've got something to contribute.

"So what's the official story about these killings?" I asked.

"Gangs. Gangs fighting a turf war over clubs. It'll make the newspapers happy. They can have plenty to say, and the pictures they'll be able to use will sell newspapers for a month. The difference is, it's all infighting between freaks. Normal people won't get upset. No one gives the mayor much of a hard time over gangs killing each other. "

"But these last two…they're not gang members. They're not freaks, either."

"In that club?" Buchanan snorted. "People won't believe that."

I didn't say anything. There wasn't anything that I felt I could say. Buchanan was trying to lump everything under a convenient heading.

The trouble was, he didn't really believe it. He'd obviously started to put together enough information to figure out there was something seriously screwy here. Whatever I might think of him, he wasn't stupid.

The colonel had said he didn't want lots of people to know about vampires, he wanted one contact. It couldn't be Buchanan. He wasn't senior enough.

And I didn't want to be on this team. Or any team with Buchanan in it. I was going to have a hell of a day until the colonel arrived.

Buchanan wasn't finished. As we were parking at the station he started speaking again. "As a team, we'll need to be real close. We'll need to know everything you know about this case." He ran a hand through his hair. "It doesn't matter if you've kinda stepped outside the bounds, huh? You're new at this. Everyone drops a ball or two. The team will look out for you. I'll look out for you."

"Of course," I said. "Nothing matters more than a quick resolution."

How dumb did he think I was? He was trying to tease information out of me. Would he and Nunez try the good cop, bad cop routine as well?

We got out and walked into the station.

"You probably don't even realize it, but something in what you know will crack this case," he went on. "I'll make sure they know it was your lead." His hand waved vaguely upstairs where the higher ranks of the police had their offices while he guided me over to his. "Use my system," he said. "I don't want anybody reading over your shoulder. I don't want anybody outside the team in on this."

I nodded and logged in on his computer to enter my statement.

"I'll get us some coffee," he said and went out.

I put my head in my hands. I was so screwed. How the hell was I going swing this? I sighed. I couldn't lie, but I couldn't be truthful either.

In the end, my statement was simply a fuller detail version of what I'd already sketched out to Buchanan and Nunez. I owned up to the scrap of paper with my number on it. Forensics would find that out anyway. Nothing about the army and vampires. I wasn't going to put anything else in a report with being ordered to by the colonel. I glanced at the clock on the screen. Another four or five hours and he would be here. I would gladly pass this mess on to him, but where was that going to leave me?

And more importantly, how many more people were going to die?

Buchanan never brought the coffee.

I'd barely finished logging off when he came back in with my report already printed. He'd probably been following me from another terminal, reading as I typed.

"Come on," he said, and jerked his head down the corridor.

He took me to an interview room. Finally, the good guy pretense was dropped. Lieutenant Morales was sitting at the table with Nunez. Buchanan tossed the report on the table and sat opposite Nunez.

"Nothing new," he said.

I was bone tired. They hadn't invited me, but I sat anyway, opposite Morales. Given the look of this, I wasn't making things any worse than they were.

Morales was running it. He had a coffee, and he took the opportunity to drink while he looked me over. He was the Denver Police golden boy. Everyone knew the position of Captain in the Major Crimes Unit was coming up in a few weeks and Morales was the anointed heir. But we also knew, all it needed was one major case to go wrong and he was out of it.

He'd want this wrapped up like a man underwater wants air.

The silence stretched. As a sergeant in Ops 4-10, I'd sat on the other side of this kind of table. Silence wasn't going to work with me. I was screwed one way or another. Every minute brought Colonel Laine closer. I picked a spot and stared at it. My spot was the vein in Morales' forehead.

"Detective Buchanan you already know," Morales said finally. "Lieutenant Nunez you've met briefly. He's with Internal Affairs. You know me presumably."

I kept my face blank and nodded. IA involvement meant they were going to try and railroad me. Everything since the drive back had been to try and get me to say something they could use in the disciplinary process.

And by telling me about Nunez, Morales was trying to get a reaction. I was determined not to give it.

What I did notice was that he didn't have the recorders on, otherwise he'd have introduced himself and me.

"At the moment, I'm chairing and this is an unofficial meeting," Morales confirmed it.

Interesting.

Buchanan stirred. I bet he'd pressed for an immediate IA case against me. He'd realized I knew things about this case that weren't in my report.

I could pull the plug now. I could demand a private conversation with a senior police officer and land everything in the colonel's lap. Or I could just say nothing. I tried to think what would serve the colonel's needs better, and regretfully arrived at the conclusion he'd want this dragged out. He'd want to be in here before Morales and others started thinking about correct procedures and authorizations. I needed delaying tactics.

"What's on the agenda, Lieutenant?" I asked.

Morales didn't like that. I was supposed to be trembling with shock. Instead I just felt tired. Tired of half-lies. Tired of walking the tightrope. Tired of walking alone.

The pulse in Morales' forehead picked up.

Buchanan couldn't restrain himself. "You don't seem to realize how serious this is—"

"What is?" I interrupted him.

Morales gestured and Buchanan shut up ungracefully.

"Why did you join the police, Farrell?" Morales said.

Because it was a job open to me that the army would allow.

Out loud, I said: "To use my skills in something worthwhile."

Morales' eyes narrowed. "Is it frustrating to you, as an army veteran with all those skills, not to be able to contribute as much as you think you can?"

I thought I could see where he was heading. He was building a case for me giving in to frustration and trying to start my own investigation. I just shrugged.

He had my folder in front of him. It would have my firearms scores and hand-to-hand reports, but, of course, it would also have my scores on legal theory.

"And you find that tempts you to sidestep things, ignore procedure? Because getting the job done is the ultimate goal?"

"Tempts me? Yes. Everyone gets tempted."

The interview wasn't going the way any of them expected. I wasn't overawed by sitting in front of senior ranks. They kept forgetting that I wasn't a fresh-faced recruit with no experience. And what they didn't know was that, short of proving I'd committed a serious felony, the power of their little courtroom procedure wouldn't mean anything when the colonel arrived. All I had to do was stick it out.

Nunez was getting as restless as Buchanan. He leaned forward to speak. Morales let him.

Nunez slipped a page from a folder and pushed it in front of me.

"Is that you?"

It was a printout of a couple of stills from the security camera on the door at Club Agonia. One with the makeup and one without.

"Yeah. That's me."

"What were you doing there?"

"Dancing." I went on the offensive. "Look, you've obviously spent a lot of time investigating me." *Instead of trying to find the murderers.* "You have some photos of me visiting a club on my day off, you've talked to my partner, got him to ask me questions. Have you got some allegations you want to make?"

Nunez ignored that. "You're saying it's entirely coincidental that you turn up at a club where two of the staff have been murdered in the same way?"

"Yes."

"Why were you at the club?" Nunez said.

"I already answered that."

"How do you know the victims?" Morales asked.

"I didn't. They were on the door in the club. I drove the girl back home."

"Is that another thing you do as a sideline?"

"What do you mean?"

Buchanan lost it. "Either you were doing bodyguard work for this club," he shouted, "or you found something out and were trying some half-witted investigation. Either way, it's your fault—"

"Shut up, Buchanan." I was shocked that Morales reprimanded him in front of me. Morales had to be completely pissed off to do that, and Buchanan knew it. He subsided.

I wasn't going to let him. It was like a little demon had taken control of my voice. "There wasn't anything to investigate, unless you think I can predict the future. And is that how you dress up to do your bodyguard work, Buchanan?" I shoved the pictures in front of him. His eyes bulged, but a look from Morales kept him quiet. Nunez got the same look.

When Morales was sure he had the meeting back under control, he turned to me again.

"So, your arrival there was coincidence. You didn't know anyone there. How is it you ended up giving an employee of the club a lift home?"

"The owner asked me. There'd been a bit of trouble earlier in the week. She asked me to drive Valery Hawks home."

"So she knows you're a policewoman?"

"Not from me. Not at that time." I glanced to the side. "But perhaps Buchanan's said something to her."

"Maybe she doesn't know your job, but she must know you to ask you to do that."

"Never met her before that night."

"That's some leap of faith she took."

It wasn't a question, so I just stared at him. He was right, but he had no clue why, and I doubted Dominé was about to tell him why she trusted me.

"You weren't there moonlighting as a bodyguard, and you weren't trying to prove you could carry out your own investigation?"

"No and no."

"And today." He flicked my report. "Acting on a call that came to you from the club's owner, you visited Ms. Hawks' apartment. You became suspicious because of the damage to the main entry door and the smell. You forced entry and called us immediately after you found her?"

"Basically correct. As I said in the report, the owner had been calling me repeatedly while I was on patrol and my personal cell phone was off. I checked it when I finished patrol and I immediately called her back."

Morales looked at Nunez. He wasn't happy, but he nodded, picked up his folder and left. IA had lost interest.

Buchanan was halfway to standing. "You can't be—"

Morales' hand slammed the table like a pistol shot. "Get out, Buchanan."

Buchanan stared at me like he wanted to strangle me right there, but he'd been given a direct order. We were not going to be friends ever, me and Detective Buchanan. Such a shame.

It was silent when they'd left.

Morales flipped open my personnel file. He picked up the first page, which was my training scores, and put that in the middle of the table. A couple of pages down, he pulled out my previous employment history and that joined the scores. From his case file, he pulled a single sheet which looked like a page full of dates and numbers. He placed that next to the others and closed the files. His cell phone joined the rest of the parade he'd set up. Then he leaned back in his chair.

"What the hell is going on, Farrell?"

"I don't understand the question, sir."

His hand came down on my employment history. "Sergeant in the military, ten year service in special operations," he said. "No negative reports. All other details classified." He jabbed at the bottom of the sheet. "That's a hell of an aura to be carrying around."

He rested his finger on the scores. "Outstanding firearms theory and practical. Lethal in hand-to-hand. Just what you'd expect from the cream of the cream in the military."

"I still don't see—"

"Because it's not what you expect from a lateral intake to the Denver PD. What the hell is a top flight soldier with a classified record doing in my patrol department?"

"Looking to be a top flight policewoman, sir." I had to assume that aspiration was history now.

"That sounded good. You should practice that, Farrell."

Okay, we could both do sarcastic.

My eyes edged towards the third page.

Morales leaned forward. "And this unbelievable rookie, she has an unbelievable random connection to an unbelievable case." He paused and tapped the third page. "What that a—" he stopped what he was going to say and tried again. "What Detective Buchanan hasn't noticed, but will eventually, is that this log of the week's security camera backups from Club Agonia happens to be missing one."

Crap.

Dominé had done what I'd asked and removed the footage I'd given the colonel. I could see why Morales was going to make that Captain spot.

I said nothing. Delaying tactics were reaching their end more quickly than I'd have liked, but Morales wasn't Buchanan. I couldn't divert him.

"What Buchanan won't know is almost exactly at the time I spotted that, I received a 9-Red-Mil notification." He pressed his cell and the calendar came up with a red bar on the afternoon. I frowned. I'd never heard of any such notification. Mil meant military, obviously.

"I had to go look it up," Morales continued. "It's a priority 'request' from the military through the Department of Defense to make myself available for a meeting."

He leaned back again and repeated himself. "What the hell is going on?"

I'd run out of delaying tactics.

"I've been operating under orders, sir, and I'll have to leave explanations to the colonel you'll be meeting shortly."

We sat looking at each other for a minute.

Morales gathered his papers and shuffled his files into a neat pile. The cell went back in his pocket and he rested his elbows on the table, clasping his hands together.

"Farrell, as of now, you are suspended pending further explanation."

Chapter 18

I drove out of the station parking lot feeling dazed. I was still in my uniform, but with no badge. Morales had had the contents of my locker delivered to me in a plastic shopping bag. I wasn't even allowed to change on the premises.

The colonel would be here in a couple more hours, so I didn't have time to sleep. Not that I would have been able to: I was too wired.

I'd get into even more trouble if I went to Club Agonia. Without thinking about it, I found the car heading back down to the site of the first murder.

The three vampires were still out here somewhere. If whatever craziness that had infected them was progressive, who knows what they could do next. I couldn't match whatever Buchanan's team were doing on searching through traffic camera videos, or hunting credit card slips or whatever. I had one line that they probably weren't pursuing.

The vampires had walked to the apartment where their first victim died. At the time, they hadn't been acting crazy. It was a fair assumption that there was a rational decision about walking. They didn't want a car linked to them to be seen at the apartment. But they wouldn't have walked for miles. They left the car somewhere where it was out of sight, or somewhere people were used to seeing it, or somewhere it wouldn't be seen.

That somewhere was in a grid of streets, no more than six by six.

But it would have been a lot for one woman to cover at the best of times.

I was driving in traffic along Speer Boulevard and visualizing the street map when a fleeting face on the sidewalk caught my eye.

Emily.

Dammit. Not only was she playing truant from school, she was all made up again. I doubted Klara had allowed her to get her hands on her cosmetics, but Emily was with a friend. I thought I recognized one of the group from the other night, mainly by her bright red hair.

I hit the brakes and got a horn blast from behind.

By the time I'd pulled over, Emily was nowhere in sight. She and her friend had to have turned down a side road, and it was one way.

I took off again, turning right, hoping to loop around and catch her, but there was no sign and fifteen minutes later, I gave up.

And if I couldn't even find one girl walking along the street, what hope did I have of finding three vampires who were hiding?

I called Werner's cell and left a voicemail.

Then I turned and headed for home. At least I could shower and change before the colonel arrived.

Chapter 19

At my apartment, I emptied the car. My police radio was in the footwell, and I'd need to remember to hand that in when they finally threw me out. I took all of it inside and tossed it on the bed with the mail while I took my shower.

I wanted to lie down and sleep. Or scream. I wasn't sure which.

I sighed.

Suck it up, Sergeant.

I switched the radio on as I dressed. It was kind of soothing. It stopped me from thinking about what was going to happen when the colonel turned up and found I was out of a job and had no lead on the vampires who were killing people in Denver.

I went through the mail. The only entertainment I got from it was scoring trash can baskets. As I crumpled and tossed, I listened with half an ear to the radio. Calls went out—domestic dispute, peeping Tom, kid with his head stuck through the bars of a fire escape. Glad I hadn't caught that one. I heard one of the rookies from my draft, Hunter, responding to a call for a second car on a traffic stop. Speer Boulevard, southbound lane near 13th. An SUV. That caught my attention—same neighborhood as the murders. And a request for a second patrol car either meant suspicious activity in the vehicle, or suspicion that the occupants might be armed. Or both.

I stopped crumpling junk mail and listened to Hunter's updates. Hunter and his partner arrived at the scene; the original patrol officers and Hunter's partner approached the vehicle.

Then all hell broke loose.

"Jesus, they're shooting out the back! Officer down! Officer down! Oh my God! They got Baker—I think he's dead—" The transmission broke off. I listened, heart in my throat.

Dispatch was saying, "All units, 13th and Speer. Shots fired. Officer down." Responses began to come in, cars giving their locations.

I grabbed my uniform and then stopped.

This didn't include me anymore. Without the badge, I was holding an ordinary dark blue shirt, not a uniform.

Still nothing from Hunter. Dispatch called out Hunter's car number. "Please respond."

I waited with everyone else, holding my breath.

Finally, Hunter came on, barely keeping it together. "Suspect vehicle heading south on Speer. Three males, one tall Caucasian, two Latino, all armed—" He took a ragged breath. "Not in pursuit. Three officers down, requesting ambulances." His voice was shaking. "It's bad."

"Ambulances en route," the dispatcher said, and then, breaking protocol, "Hang in there, Hunter."

There was another long, shaky pause. Then, "Request additional ambulance. I've got a girl, twelve years old, broke out of the back of the SUV during the firefight. Possible abduction…" There was a faint, high-pitched voice in the background, and then Hunter said, "Oh my God. They've got another one still in there." He took a deep breath, trying his damnedest to be professional. "Proceed with caution. SUV may contain a kidnap victim. Female, Caucasian, twelve years old, dark hair, Goth makeup."

Emily. Had to be. Oh, God, Emily.

I reached for my gun. It was my personal firearm and I was licensed, so it hadn't been taken with the badge. It was a Walther 9mm, a good little gun, but not what I wanted now.

From under my bed, I pulled out the heavy safe and opened it. Inside was my handgun from my days in Ops 4-10. It was a Heckler & Koch Mark 23 SOCOM. If I wanted targets to stay hit, the .45 rounds from this were the ones to do the job.

I took the radio too and left at a run, past my startled landlady. I leaped into my car and thanked my lucky stars that I'd fixed the engine.

As I drove past Gerritsen, I saw the cruisers outside the Schumachers' and heard more details coming in on the radio. The SUV had disappeared. That wouldn't last. In a city like Denver, you can't disappear for long. The press had been listening too, and there were vans all over. They might get in the way, but at least they were extra eyes on the streets.

To everyone else, it was 'just' an abduction. Negotiators would be sitting down in situation rooms. Buchanan's team might be linking it to the murders and puzzling over the significance.

I was the only person in the city who knew the three men were vampires, and that something had sent them over the edge. I was the only one who knew Emily wouldn't last long enough for the negotiators to save her.

I left the car at the south end of Bannock and started trotting a search pattern. I was gambling with Emily's life, relying on my instinct that somewhere in the triangular grid of streets between Speer, 13th and Bannock, there was a place where an SUV had parked off the road and out of sight.

And Valerie gave it to me.

"...pretty as a picture, he'd hang me on his wall. The next one said I should be in a gallery..."

I could hear her voice telling me that Rodrigo had stopped the other two. But not because he didn't want them teasing her. Because he didn't want them talking about the gallery. Not *a* gallery, *the* gallery.

Galería del Sur was closed down for refurbishment.

It lay at the south end of Cheyenne: a narrow, tall building, set back from the road between two offices. And it had a basement parking garage with a steel door on it.

There was nothing to see through the lobby doors; they had been boarded over, but lights gleamed inside the building through the cracks between boards.

I tried the garage door. It was solid. But not solid enough to stop a faint, brassy smell of vampire from drifting out.

Chapter 20

I ran through the office next door, ignoring the frantic calls from the receptionist. I found a way out into their parking space that backed onto the gallery. It was too much to hope for a door to the gallery that had been left open, but at least there were windows I could see through.

One of them was open on a latch, letting air circulate. I crouched down out of sight and gave it a quiet shake, but it was too strong to force open. Peering over the sill, I couldn't see any movement inside. But I could hear men arguing, and a child crying.

The receptionist appeared at the office's back door and was about to step out into the parking lot. I got the HK out of the shoulder holster. The thing is huge—there is no way she couldn't see what it was. Her hand flew to her mouth and she disappeared back into the building, slamming the door shut behind her.

She'd be calling 911. Good. I pulled the police radio out and tried beating her to it.

"This is Officer Farrell. I'm in a parking lot behind Galería del Sur, on Cheyenne. I have reason—"

The radio squalled in the way it does when someone tries to override you.

"Farrell, you're suspended, you stupid bitch. Get the fuck off the radio." Buchanan's voice was distorted by his screaming into the microphone.

I closed my eyes and paused, then went on. "I have reason to believe the kidnappers of Emily Schumacher are in the gallery. I'm requesting immediate situation team on site."

"Farrell—"

There was a choked-off noise followed by silence, then the dispatcher came back. "Got that, situation team alerted." He'd passed the buck to whoever was running the team.

A minute passed and I found out who that was. Morales' voice came on. "Farrell, are you sure?" At least he wasn't debating my current employment status with the police.

"Yes, Lieutenant. I can hear them arguing, and I can hear her crying."

"The team is on its way. You keep back and you do not do anything."

The vampires had gotten it together enough to get out of sight. If they were rational enough for that, their argument might be about how the hell they were going to get away now. They wouldn't be aware that I was here, or a SWAT team was on the way. As far as they were concerned, their best bet would be to split up and walk away.

They wouldn't leave any witnesses if they did that.

Only a few minutes, but it might be too late when the SWAT team arrived.

I was trained in hostage rescue. Certainly well trained enough to know that going in with a single handgun, no other weapons or distraction, no Kevlar vest, and no other protection was 'outside parameters,' as my instructors had put it. Meaning it would likely get me killed and almost certainly get Emily killed too.

It was hot, crouched down next to the window. My senses seemed sharpened. I could hear the dull roar of the ventilation fans from the office across the parking lot, the cars passing in the street, music blaring from one. I had the feeling of time slipping through my fingers, like dreams on waking.

What would Top do?

Master Sergeant Gabriel Luther Wells had been my touchstone in Ops 4-10. Any combat situation where I had time to think, I figured out what he would do, then did it.

I could almost hear him now, his deep, steady voice calming me.

I'd once asked him what he was afraid of. His reply had been succinct—*failure*. If I went into the gallery and failed today, I was unlikely to be in a position to regret it. And one thing he couldn't advise me on was vampires.

The smell of them was oozing from the building, as if all their emotions made their scent thick as fog. It was a sickly, brassy smell. The word *vampire* pounded in my head in time with my heartbeat. The sort of creature that had bitten me in the jungle. The sort that had killed my squad. The ones who'd killed Valerie. And Marcel. My breath came quicker.

"Listen, Farrell, the SWAT team will be there in five minutes. Just hold on. Do *not* precipitate anything. Do *not* go in that building. These people are trained for this sort of situation."

So am I.

"I can't hear you, Farrell."

"I heard what you said." I was never going to get away with that evasion with Morales; he was too smart.

"Farrell, you stay where you are. You have no backup. Those men are armed. They have killed two policemen already—"

"Hold it. They're shouting now." I strained to make it out. "I don't like this."

It started with one of them shouting, and now all three were going at it. Some argument about getting away.

"Farrell, you will stay outside." Morales was shouting too, the radio distorting his voice.

Emily screamed.

My sight locked down. Everything seemed crystal clear and somehow distant. I dropped the radio. It bounced on the sidewalk, buzzing with noises that meant nothing. The main door was too far away, too obvious, too secure. Emily had run out of time. The sick bastards had picked her for a snack and were getting ready to run away. They wouldn't be taking Emily with them.

I rocked back and looked at the window I'd been crouching beneath. I wasn't really planning. I had no idea what the building looked like inside, or where they were. I had nothing. It didn't matter. I hurled myself at the window and exploded through it.

Glass was still falling as I rolled and came up with the HK in front of me. The first vampire was there, standing over Emily. He was turning, his face a mask of surprise. I fired. Tap, tap, tap. The way I had been taught in Ops 4-10. Chest, chest, head, and I didn't miss at that distance.

Target Antonio down said a calm, slow voice in my mind. *Two targets and nine rounds remaining.*

Ten yards further in, Rodrigo leaped up an open frame set of stairs to snatch a shotgun from a pile of gear. Mistake. The only thing that would stop me was a threat to Emily, and she was lying on the floor behind Antonio's corpse, screaming, but well out of the way. I sprinted at Rodrigo, fired one shot as he ducked. My bullet went wide. I vaulted the railing rather than climb the stairs.

He backpedalled and fired. I felt the breath of the shotgun blast and fired back. I wasn't stationary, and even close up it's very difficult to sprint and shoot a handgun. I was lucky that the bullet tore at his thigh.

"Shit!" He was distracted enough. The shotgun wasn't on me. I stopped and steadied. The first of my intended three round burst hit him in the shoulder and I held the second as he spun backwards. The shotgun went off again but his aim was wild. Even hit, he moved unnervingly quickly.

He dived behind a partition.

I ran forward and jumped, tucking myself in a ball and rolling as I hit the ground. I came up into a crouch, both hands on the HK. Tap, tap, tap. Shit, he was so quick. I missed with the head shot. I had a flashback from the jungle, my team firing and missing, firing and missing. Figures like shadows in the trees.

Never make yourself a stationary target. Avoid moving where you're expected. I leaped to one side.

Raul was on the next flight of stairs up. He had a shotgun as well and he fired into the area between me and Rodrigo. I snapped a shot off at Raul to keep him occupied as I jinked again.

Rodrigo was still fighting, trying to get a clear shot even while his life blood was spurting from chest wounds. His hands shook, trying to steady. The shotgun roared again, missed, and now I was close enough. I slammed him against the wall, breaking ribs. His hand convulsed and the shotgun fired into the ceiling. His blood was all over me, spurting from wounds and spraying from his mouth as we struggled. Then I rammed the HK under his jaw and blew the back of his head off.

I twisted around, holding his body as a shield, but Raul was running. Up.

I pulled the Remington pump action from Rodrigo's dead hands. It was empty. I threw it aside.

One target and two rounds remaining.

I ran for the stairs.

The shotgun blasted a huge dent in the metal step I'd just passed.

And again. He couldn't hit me, but I couldn't get a clear shot at him.

He was on the top floor. Was there a fire escape? He turned to look for the exit and I got my first solid shot off at him, up through the railings. I hit his calf. Straight through the muscle; I missed the bone or it would have blown him over.

He swore and lurched around to fire again.

Last bullet. I squeezed off a shot, but I was ducking as the shotgun came to bear on me again.

I dropped the HK at the same time as I heard the click of his pin on an empty chamber, and I was on him even as he tried to use the shotgun like a club.

With his leg useless, he couldn't push back against me. I lifted him. We were staggering across the room, picking up speed. There was a panoramic window in front of us.

I stopped. He didn't.

I saw him clearly, in shocking detail amidst the sparkling shards of glass. The exact point at which it registered with him that he was about to die, the widening of the eyes. The scream. An age later, the thud and the sudden silence.

I ran back down. It seemed much further. Five floors. The end of the adrenaline rush made me weak.

Emily screamed again when she saw me. I realized what I must look like, but I couldn't help that.

"They're gone, Emily," I said, trying to soothe her. "All gone."

"Amber?"

I pulled my bloody jacket off and hugged her to me.

There were bullhorns sounding outside.

She was sobbing as I sat us down.

"Shhh. It's okay. It's okay," I said. I was trembling with the aftereffects of adrenaline. "You're safe now. I've got you.

The police are outside. They don't know what's happened. It'll be noisy and frightening when they come in, but you're safe now."

"Don't leave me."

"I won't. We'll go out together. Let's just lie down here on the floor, okay? Close your eyes and cover your ears."

We lay down.

Even with our precautions, the thunder and lightning of the stun grenades was disorienting. Emily cried, the noise thin, and I hugged her back against me as the SWAT team came pouring in. They were in full gear: Kevlar armor, helmets and black masks. They came from three sides at once, yelling and shouting, streaming up the stairs like large, murderous ants.

A couple of them pulled at our arms, trying to separate us. Emily refused; she wasn't letting go and they let us stay together as they hauled us to our feet. With a shield of four of them pressed close around us, we were hurried through the shattered front door, Emily's face hidden in my shirt, wetting it with her tears.

We stumbled out into a strange, frozen silence. There were police cars scattered across the road, officers with guns crouched behind them. To one side an ambulance and the SWAT team transport waited, dwarfed by an armored army truck with its doors tightly closed.

Morales and Buchanan were standing in a group of uniformed police beside the truck. So was Colonel Laine. Our eyes met and the colonel gave me the smallest nod.

Medics pulled us into the ambulance. I shrugged off their attentions. As they closed the doors, I saw Knight's face in the sea of blue shirts.

He raised his hand and said something. It might have been "well done, partner."

Chapter 21

TUESDAY

I drove west, out to Red Rocks, and parked where I got a view back over Denver.

With the car door open I crossed my legs and rested my feet on the sill. Warm fall air blew across me, carrying with it the promise of coolness to come.

Morales and the colonel had held an emergency meeting, slamming down a news blackout around the case until Morales' carefully worded press conference.

Today's papers had run a great story. Gangs running successful underground clubs. Outsiders muscling in, killing staff, trying to take over. Police following clues, closing in. Hitmen cornered in a building, taking a child hostage. A textbook, surgical strike by the SWAT team. A neat, orderly operation all wrapped up. Move on folks, nothing to see here.

I'd mutually agreed with the police to resign, apparently, not that any newspapers bothered with that supposedly unrelated footnote.

Morales had praise showered on him from on high. Scuttlebutt said he'd been given the Captain slot in Major Crimes last night. He knew everything the army knew about me now, and had requested for me to be on call for him as a consultant. At least no one else in the police seemed to know, though he'd already said he would have to build a team in case of emergencies and they'd have to be briefed.

The colonel disappeared with the squad before anyone started asking questions about a tooled-up military team wandering around Denver. He was coming back for a meeting with me at the end of the week. Maybe that was how much time I had left free. Morales asking for me to be on call wasn't the same as the army agreeing to it.

Club Agonia was gone. I'd walked into the echoing building with a profound sense of unreality. The entrance with the mechanized head was gone, nothing but a gaping hole left. They'd opened up huge shuttered windows on the upper floors and stripped all the black glass panels already. Bright sunbeams slanted across the empty shell, turning the dusty air into a slow honey. Workers were noisily dismantling the giant frames that had held the look-through glass while others carried stock out to waiting trucks. I saw Dominé's elegant desk and chairs stacked in a corner, waiting for loading.

It all looked so everyday, almost tawdry, like a stage magician's props exposed to the glare of sunlight. As if everything had been an illusion. My fingers ran over the skin of my neck, and I felt a prickle of pressure. No, not all illusion.

The site manager hurried over and shepherded me out. "It's not safe in here, ma'am," he said. I snorted.

As I started to move away, someone called.

"Ms. Farrell?"

I turned. It was difficult to be sure, but I thought it was the highwayman who had brought champagne for us in Dominé's office. He was in jeans and a sweatshirt, looking like the college kid he probably was.

"I wasn't sure it was you," he said, stumbling over the words. He meant I wasn't dressed as a vampire. "Dominé thought you might come."

I gave him a tight, polite smile, which was as much as I could manage. "She's not here?"

"She's gone on to Albuquerque," he said. "We're moving." He mumbled and waved a hand at the building. "Well, obviously."

I sighed. "I came to tell her I'm sorry. I failed."

He turned his head aside and nodded. He took an envelope from his pocket. "She left this for you."

Inside was her card with her cell number. There was no written message. Pinned through the top corner was a single, shiny barb from an *angoisse*.

I got out of the car and sat cross-legged on the hood to take full advantage of the breeze. Between Dominé and Master Liu, I'd had my fill of mysterious warnings and messages this last week. I needed to keep it simple. There were things going on in my head and my body that I'd have to deal with. The opportunity to do that would be a privilege. Just at the moment, my head was full of staying human, free and sane. They all felt intimately related.

I cradled Tara's plaque in my hands.

"Wow, that's a happy face," said Tara. *"Fill me in."*

"Oh, let me see. I screwed up and a girl died because I wasn't going to risk losing my job crying wolf. Which job, by the way, I lost anyway. I blew away three vampires, so the army's pissed at me, because they wanted to have a little chat with them. I've breached the secrecy terms of my agreement, so I bet the army's legal department wants me shot. Morales knows about me. The rest of the police, well, God knows what they think. Maybe that I'm some kind of mutant soldier experiment that escaped from a laboratory. Half of them are probably pissed at the army for doing that to me and the other half at the army for letting me out."

"Or both."

"Or both. Don't interrupt when I'm sobbing." I sighed. "The colonel hasn't had me hauled back to base. Yet. That's the real good news. He's not going to get me another job, so what do I do? I've got to get a job, even if it's cashier at McDonald's. On the big assumption that I'm allowed to stay here, whatever job I get, I'm still going to be working for the army, for expenses and peanuts, *and* I'm expected to be available as a consultant for Morales. He hasn't even got any peanuts, so I guess I'm doing that pro bono."

"Who's Bono? Not the singer?"

"Not funny. Where am I going to get a job that lets me drop everything to go chasing vampires for the police *and* the army?"

"Doh! You have a job offer."

"I *had* a sort of job offer. That was on Monday. Today is Tuesday."

"Call."

Sane advice, given it came from a voice in my head.

I called Whitman.

"Mr. Whitman, it's Amber Farrell. I'm sorry about missing the call yesterday. It got kinda busy at the station."

"No problem, Amber, no problem. Y'know, you could make my day brighter…"

"Yeah, about that, Mr. Whitman. I…ah…I'd like to come in and talk about it."

"That's great! Fantastic! Look, I'm in meetings until silly time tonight. Come in first thing tomorrow, nine o' clock?"

"Will do."

"That's great," he said again. "Talk tomorrow."

"Looking forward to it. Bye," I said, trying to get the tone right as I ended the call. Positive, upbeat. Yeah!

I'd have to practice that. If I actually got clients, I'd have to make nice. I shuddered, and while the cell was in my hand, I decided I'd better make the next call before I lost my nerve.

"Mom, hi."

"Amber! This is a pleasant surprise. Is it one of your days off?"

"Uh, not quite."

"Hmm." There was some background noise. "Well, dear, I'm sitting down. You can tell me now."

"I've left the police."

"Oh, that's—" she managed to stop herself from saying how wonderful it was, "—interesting. What are you going to do instead? Back to accounting? There's this firm John knows—"

"I have...um...the thing is, I think I'm going to be a private investigator," I blurted out.

"Let's not be too hasty here," she said, hastily. "You're under no pressure to get a new job, Amber. You know you can come and stay anytime. Heaven knows, I owe you so much—"

"Thanks, Mom, but I need this. Really, it's okay. It's safer than being an accountant."

"Exactly how did you come up with that?"

"Okay, it was off the top of my head. But I don't think it's like the PI shows on TV. It's not that exciting."

I hadn't changed her opinion, even after another fifteen minutes. I'd never be able to explain to her. The best I could do was guide her generally in the direction of my needing my independence, and wanting a job that didn't mean too much time behind a desk.

The truth about my life, the threat of the prions in my body, the obligations to the army and the police? Those I'd never be able to explain to her, even if I wanted to.

Far away in front of me, edges softened by the haze, lay Denver.

Sure as taxes, there were vampires down there. A community that had been hidden for who knows how long. And the army wanted me to find out all about them. In my free time.

There were roads down there as well. I-70 would take me to Kansas, I-25 to Cheyenne, I-76 and I-80 to Omaha. I pictured the network of roads spreading out like rivers across the land, full of little backwaters where I could hide. I could do it. I'd been trained by the best. It would be the easier option. But what would I say, as I-80 took me past North Platte and the biggest railroad junction in the country?

Sorry, Valerie.

And how many Valeries might be out there, now and in the future?

I drove back down into the city and went to the Schumachers' shop, on the off chance they were around.

Werner was. Klara was with Emily and had sent Werner back to look after the shop. Emily was having another session down at the station. Rules dictated they had to give her plenty of breaks. Quite how they were explaining the need for the real story of what happened in the gallery to be secret, I didn't know.

I got a big hug from Werner and a suspicion of shiny eyes.

Regardless of the reason he was there, he closed the shop, and insisted I stay until Emily got back, bribing me with coffee and cookies. As if that would work.

Then, when I was sitting down in his little kitchen area, he brought out a box.

"These," he said, "these are for you, and this is my guarantee. Never, never so long as we live, will you not have a pair of my boots to wear."

They were beautiful. Handmade cowboy boots, lower in the heel than some, so I could wear them even when I was working. There was a matching belt. They were my unique design, my very own, that he said he would never make for anyone else.

Call me shallow. I put them on and felt better.

Raw Deal is the prequel of the
Bite Back series
Continue with
Bite Back 1 : Sleight of Hand

Reader feedback for Sleight of Hand:
"I couldn't put it down!"
"This book was a blast!"
"I can't wait until the next one!"
"Loved it, loved it, loved it."

Purchase Sleight of Hand:
US Amazon – http://www.amazon.com/Sleight-Hand-Bite-Back-ebook/dp/B008RJXPQM/
UK Amazon – http://www.amazon.co.uk/Sleight-Hand-Bite-Back-ebook/dp/B008RJXPQM/
DE Amazon – http://www.amazon.de/Sleight-Hand-Bite-Back-ebook/dp/B008RJXPQM/
CA Amazon – http://www.amazon.ca/Sleight-Hand-Bite-Back-ebook/dp/B008RJXPQM/

Series ongoing with:
Bite Back 2 : Hidden Trump
Bite Back 3 : Wild Card

Email Mark@Athanate.com to get an
alert email when
Bite Back 4 is published.